I DROPPED MY LEFT WING, PULLED WITH MY RIGHT, AND NOW THE FALLS FLEXED BELOW ME.

Up! Cup and pull, cup and pull, cup and pull. The firm full muscle pull exhilarated. I was much stronger than her, but after several beats she still flew easily above my shoulder.

"Fly, mud-man, fly!"

Fly we did. The falls sparkled behind us. Several hundred feet below us curved greenery and garden, endless intricacies of greens, purples, tans, and browns, delicately punctuated by flower beds rainbowing through reds, yellows, and blues. Ahead of us rose the great growth of Tree-elbow's master-pieces, a tree — the tree — whose sprouts soared small every-where behind us, a tree that here rose and spread several thousand feet.

The air breezed my sweating arms. The sky's blue darkened precipitously into steely purple and I glimpsed stars along the horizon.

Suddenly, out of illusion, appeared the silicon vault of heaven!

D1555466

Also by Justin Leiber published by Tor Books

BEYOND HUMANITY
THE SWORD AND THE EYE
THE SWORD AND THE TOWER

JUSTIN LEIBER

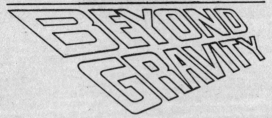

BEYOND GRAVITY

TOR®

A TOM DOHERTY ASSOCIATES BOOK
NEW YORK

BEYOND GRAVITY

A TOR Book
Published by Tom Doherty Associates, Inc.
49 West 24 Street
New York, N.Y. 10010

Cover art by Mark Maxwell

ISBN: 0-812-54435-8   Can. ISBN: 0-812-54436-6

Library of Congress Catalog Card Number: 88-50344

First edition: September 1988

Printed in the United States of America

0 9 8 7 6 5 4 3 2 1

"I wonder if I've been changed in the night? Let me think: was I the same when I got up this morning? I almost think I can remember feeling a little different. But if I'm not the same, the next question is, Who in the world am I?

"I'm sure I'm not Ada," she said, "for her hair goes in such long ringlets, and mine doesn't go in ringlets at all; and I'm sure I can't be Mabel, for I know all sorts of things, and she, oh, she knows such a very little! Besides, *she's* she, and *I'm* I, and—oh, dear, how puzzling it all is! I'll try if I know all things I used to know. Let me see: four times five is twelve, and four times six is thirteen, and four time seven is—oh, dear! I shall never get to twenty at that rate!"

Alice in Wonderland

1 _____

Drifting. Drifting. Rolling slowly now, head over heels in the womblike darkness, silence and the distant hush, hush sound of air, in and out, in and out, in and out more slowly. Slowly. Must get ... Slowly, dreamidown, down, down, done.

I DON'T KNOW which was worse, when I woke up. What I did find. Or what I didn't. What I did find was a monkey—bent over, looking down at me. You know the kind. Slender, long, lithe body. Lean, long arms, legs, and tail. Straight, sleek, white hair all over except for the black face, and the black palms and soles.

Only this version was six feet tall, its head gigantic on such a slender frame. Only the eyes—those ancient glittering eyes, twice human-size—looked down on me with the wisdom, penetration, and total assurance of an Apollonian god.

1

A millisecond sufficed to take in the too tall monkey, who stared down at me with deep brown eyes, twice human-size. My realization that I didn't know who I was took longer. Thirty seconds. The mind moves fast, especially when fear holds the whip. (And you understand I recount this in retrospect, a civil reconstruction of what flashed through me at the time.)

What I didn't find was myself. I didn't know who I was.

I couldn't think of my parents or my schools or any job I'd held or place I'd lived. I *felt* that I'd had all of these, that I was somehow an ordinary twenty-second-century human being. But when I tried to come up with specifics, my mind refused to make sense of the question, like a restricted-user computer that fires back "syntax error" however you phrase a vital question. *I didn't know my own name.* Even my body seemed somehow unfamiliar.

"Your servant, sir," said the sleek-haired, human-tall, skeletal-lean monkey. "Welcome to Vineland." He spoke English with an impeccable, antique accent. I saw his lips, a mingling border of pink and seal-brown fringed by silver fur, that express, mouth, phrase—that *make* the words I hear. I shook, shook all over. Arms flailed. The long muscles of my back convulsed. My teeth chattered.

He touched my belly with a small glassy

2

staff. My muscles stilled. Warmth spread. Calm spread with it, though my mind shrieked.

"Oh dear, oh dear," he said. "I hoped we might start better than that." His voice was thin and high-pitched, with a slight lisp.

I heard that voice croon the beginning of "Rock-a-bye-baby" as the warm darkness closed. When the bough breaks, I go down too.

My last thoughts were these. I felt light beyond the influence of his drug. I was nearly weightless. Why hadn't I noticed this from the moment of waking?

I WOKE MORE slowly and fully the next time around. My first waking seemed now like dream or nightmare, like fog that daylight will burn clear.

Some part of me announced that I must not open my eyes or move a muscle until I understand more. Of course, I tell myself, the weird tall monkey-man, and not knowing who I am, all that was just dream and dream remnants. I'll come full awake in just a second. But meanwhile I'll play this game.

Or, maybe, there's more to it—*is this part of the dream game?*—maybe my head got hit and

4

blood leaked in my brain, and I can't get things straight yet. There aren't any giant monkeys at all, let alone ones that act like wise physicians. If Vegan slug moss makes you see flying lions and alcohol makes you see pink elephants, surely there's something that makes you see slender man-sized langur monkeys.

A stroke could have closed up some blood vessels in my brain with the same effect. Let's see. Any close relatives with circulatory disease?

You don't . . .

What's my normal blood pressure?

Let's not worry about the fact that you can't think of relatives or your blood.

I knew that I was human. My mind full with knowledge of the orderly, crowded hustle and bustle of modern North American life, of frizzies and flickers and hologrammic statues. My memories gave me a sense that I'd grown up in the Southwest, though I also felt I might not have been there recently. I knew the answers to the questions they ask you to tell whether your brain is so old or smashed up that you're gaga— all the way from Lord Asano is the eleventh President of the Ecological Syndics to the fact that the Houston Cougars won the 2109 Solar Spaceball Series from the Titan Tigers. Why couldn't I remember my name?

Come on, maybe it's some drug I took, or one someone slipped me. And it could be some chemical solvent loose in the air, or maybe the air in my ship was helox, low pressure, and the circulation went dead—you don't notice oxygen lack then, with no carbon dioxide in the mix to make you gasp.

I was weightless.

That much I was sure of. You know the old joke about the spacer, who's back on earth after years and years away from the terra-all-too-firma. Spacer says, "I did feel it was a touch hard to breathe. But when I did a flip-roll to put me across the compartment into the kitchen bay, and found the floor squashed into my nose, then I knew I was back on mother tit."

—Damn, you don't even know what sex you are—

But just the slightest shoulder twitch floated me up a couple of inches, until the straps held me and tidily eased me back into a sleek furry surface that molded itself against the back and sides of my body like a loving mother round her baby. Most comfortable bunk I'd ever run into.

And, of course . . .

Was anything of course now?—

I was male. I felt pressure in my penis. Common enough when a guy wakes up. Still, like everything else, it felt strange.

I knew my ABC's, calculus, space suit drill, my Chomsky hierarchy of grammars, the capital cities of the sixty-three states of North Amer-

6

ica (well, most of them, anyhow), and the five navigable black holes—wormholes—that allow interstellar travel. I knew that it was early in 2110. (I was two years short about that.) My body was my body. *How could it not be?* And still, like everything else, it felt strange.

But what could be meant by "strange"? It's what doesn't fit. And "doesn't fit" has got to mean what doesn't fit with any of the memories, ideas, or feelings that make up a reasonably normal human being. And, even assuming you are a reasonably normal human being, you can't get to the core of those memories, ideas, and feelings. You don't know whether something's really strange to *you* until you find out who, and what, you are.

One thing was for sure. The world I remembered didn't have man-sized monkeys in it, especially man-sized monkeys who speak English like a twentieth-century gentleman. But feelings are hard to get a detailed grip on. Lots of things feel strange, like when you cross your fingers and rub between them with the first finger of the other hand.

Maybe you're crazy, maybe nothing fits. Maybe you don't know what fits or doesn't anymore.

Nothing wrong with trying. I argue well enough with myself. Something always doesn't fit in. Like the philosopher said, reality is set us as a task. You don't get it for free.

I hope, I hope, I hope this is the damnedest hangover I've ever had.

A, B, C, D, E, F, G—Okay, already. We're playing this game. Not quite awake and I pretend to figure out where I am, or what's happened. You've played this game as a kid. Use your senses. Start with A.

A. Like little Alice, I have fallen and continue to fall down a hole in the ground. Objection: I am falling—I am weightless, that is—but not through anything. My ears tell me that nothing near is shooting by me. What's around me is in free-fall with me.

B. Horrible hangover or accident? But I don't feel the headache and cotton-mouth. Just like you can tour your body, relaxing one muscle set at a time, you can survey yourself without visible motion. My arms and hands, legs and feet, all complete. I can even feel my coccyx, though I have no tail like that gigantic dream monkey. I can twitch my face and ears, and move my scalp. Seems like I have a full head of hair and no bandages in it.

C. Like Asteroid Sally, I've been kidnapped by the venomous Venusians, who have implanted my mind in an octopus and played the mind tapes of Ulgar Fangborn into my innocent brain. Remember how she

8

got out of that one? Objection: I can't feel my tentacles. Moreover, after the implant, Ulgar Fangborn always smelled "the stench of innocence" from his new body. And what I smell is garden, the faint, sweet smell of trees and scrub and moss, in open air, without the inevitable smell of human waste esters that hydroponic systems carry.

D. The monkeys of Oz's wicked witch have captured me. I know well enough what suggests that ancient children's story. But my dream monkey was man-sized and wingless. And besides, no little dog Toto, and I'm an adult male, not Dorothy.

Enough. I must take a peek. One casual blink now and the baddies wouldn't catch me.

JUST ONE blink. Eyes again shut before the startlement. Drink the outlines in the afterimage.

Soft-looking, light-colored wood. A light, high-roofed, airy chamber whose walls had the grace and irregularity of natural growth, gently smoothed and cleaned, no bark, leaf, or sprig. A large, smoothly curved window nestled into the wooden curves. Through it, a glimpse of bamboo shoots.

Your tropical paradise hologrammic fantasy projection, number one. No wonder I dreamt a man-sized monkey to go with it. Or maybe the monkey was part of the illusion.

And even at a blink, what a rich illusion. None of the sparkle that was the telltale of holograms. I was in a very expensive psychiatric institution or a very expensive whorehouse. Bring on the dancing interns.

But one blink leads to another. And another. The illusion was magnificent. Fulfilled our deepest childhood dream. The tree whose lower reaches formed a cozy nest, impossibly high, airy, and well lit, doubtless scrubbed and buffed clean by squads of industrious elves. Banzai bonsai. Even under a careful stare, none of the usual hologrammic pinpoint rainbow flickers.

The bamboo alone showed movement. The slender, emerald leaves, longer and more slender than I've ever seen, swayed gently, languorously, as if disturbed by some Hollywood tropical breeze, too slow and viscous for real air. Slow-motion holograms.

But, in weightlessness, things could move like that. And the light movement from the wondrous slender bamboo was not like hologrammatic sparkle. It was the perfect illusion of the play of sunlight on greenery. Hello, madness!

My hand moved up before my face toward that oh-so-real wall. You know how, when you "touch" most partition holograms, they're set to wiggle, shimmer, and disappear, like a still pond in which you see a forest scene waver and flicker out in the turbulence created by your hand. Convenient, so you don't trip over a toi-

11

let, or whatever the hologram happens to mask. If you're like most of us—like me—you flinch just a bit when you "touch," as if you might get a shock.

My hand moved up before my face toward that oh-so-real surface, with the light, delicate look of balsa, the color of teak, and the graceful asymmetry of untouched nature.

My hand slammed back into my forehead. The wall was there, as solid as oak and as real as your mama's breast. That was the way it felt, and felt so strong there's no denying.

I reached forward once more. Slow. Should I . . . ?

"By all means, sir, please feel free to touch it. A pleasant material." Returned from dream, I heard once more the courtly, then, high-pitched lisp of the Apollonian monkey.

"From Tau Ceti III, originally." Once more I saw the black face of the slender, man-tall monkey. The twice human-sized wise brown eyes engulfed me. His body covered with shimmering, sleek white hair except for the black palm and fingers, with which he gestured to take in the chamber.

"Brought to civilization some thousands of years ago. Our tree is young, for she was but a seedling fifty years ago. Tree-elbow's masterwork."

I took some time to fully understand these last three sentences. The planetary name "Tau

Ceti III" came from a mechanical translator, as did the word "Tree-elbow." Both voiced in ISBM unisex alto, as the lordly monkey made the original piccololike sounds in the background, the rest of his sentences univocally issued through his thin, pink-black monkey lips with his courtly English lisp.

Astonishment overwhelmed fear.

IV _____

"**C**OME, NOW, do touch it, touch the wood. You need to make contact with the concrete things around you."

Under his patient instruction, my hand went back. The wall certainly felt like wood, the roughness and irregularity of light bark covering what seemed to be a living tree—a tree that made rooms, that grew around the glass of windows.

"Tree-elbow's creation, with the contribution of the tree itself, of course. Call me Kagu. Per-

14

mit me to show you our world." He bowed and touched his right hand to his lips.

Tentatively and slowly, I raised myself up and sat. Not quite weightlessness. In this world I weighed perhaps a dozen pounds. Kagu, given his lean frame, must weigh half of that. Convenient to have some weight if only to keep things in place without grabbers. Couldn't tell whether this was real gravity or the effect of rotation. Was this a real or an artificial world?

"Please." He gestured toward where the chamber's woody expanse seemed to create a natural, not-quite-rectangular exit.

Kagu lacked covering, aside from a couple of small devices attached to his left arm. I could see he was male. I had on a blue utility coverall—what you see on a mechanic or engineer. I wanted to check the labels to see if they mentioned someplace familiar.

I managed to stand without dizziness or float. My face felt flushed.

Now Kagu's manner was so easy, so assured, that he had me through the door—indeed, helped me through, with a brief touch of his slender fingers on my back—before I thought to question him. And when I came to the other side of the door, all questions evaporated into what I saw.

Imagine a blue so intense, a sky so pure and absolute, that you feel lost in it—sucked, seduced, enraptured—into its endless airy embrace. Imagine trees, trees cleaner, lighter, taller, more delicate than any you've seen. The knobby curlicues that made the room we'd left sweep upward in fantastic woody eddies and streamers, daubed here and there by balconies and ramparts of greenery, all formed a tree the size of a mountain, its highest branches lost in the blue distance, its girth stretched in all directions, with rainbows of flowers and exotic fungi that punctuated the whole.

Long, thin fingers gently smoothed my shoulder. "I had hoped that you would find it beautiful," softly entoned Kagu. "You will enjoy today's sunset, I think. Tree-elbow, again. His last work, I fear. Rain and rainbows at the very least. He became broadbrush at the end." All this I heard in his soft lisp except for "Tree-elbow" and "broadbrush," which issued from the wristwatch-sized translator on his arm.

"What am I—" I began, shrugging off his hand, trying to shake off the dreamlike calm that held me.

"Now, now," said Kagu, "it is not yet time to ask important questions. All in good time. We are late for our appointment with Nod and Nelly. Come."

He set off down a white-graveled path, his arms swung back-and-forth in the "swimming gait" favored by low-gravity walkers. I followed.

V _____

T HOUGH HE was tall, large-headed, and delicately built, Kagu set a graceful but brisk pace. Here and there his long tail reached out to briefly grasp a shoot, easing his way through a sharp turn. While I found it reasonably easy to adjust to a twelve-pound walking weight, it was all I could do to keep up with him.

In any case, the extraordinary greenery, punctuated in places by white gravel and moss-daubed rock, stifled my questions. Image a vast garden, miles in extent. Imagine each hillock, each glen, each bamboo stand or fern patch, carefully and brilliantly designed by Japanese master gardener—and then freshened and swept clean on a daily basis. In the distance I began to see the misted top of a waterfall and beyond that, against the distant blue, several winged creatures soared in the lazy manner of raptors, though they looked like bats.

A few minutes later, we turned off the main path. A few yards found us at a woody enclosure, as if the immense tree that was "Tree-elbow's masterpiece" had blown a bubble of wood, whose undersurface had shaped itself into comfortable depressions. Two younger versions of Kagu looked up from within.

"Nod and Nelly," said Kagu, extending his palm toward one and then the other, "permit me to introduce the human. May we join you?" Kagu took my shoulder again as the two other monkeys rose.

Nod was male, his penis more full than Kagu's. Yet his youthfulness, his sleeker fur and pinker lips, somehow more emphasize the frailness of his build. He extended his left hand toward me, showed his white teeth, and lisped something like, "Butter dar, bard."

I took his thin, long-fingered paw. The nails look dark pink, palm and fingers black. I let him draw my hand in several sweeps, up and down. I felt a mixture of terror and apathy. I didn't know who I was or what this was. My

18

stomach surged up my throat. If I looked as bad as I felt, I looked terrible.

"Gooddah meetcha, bard," said Nod. He showed his teeth again and launched into the piccolo chirping that seemed to be normal monkey speech. Kagu reached over to touch the wristwatch-sized device on Nod's arm.

"Sorry, forgot to turn my talk-box on" said Nod—or rather, the translational device said that, concurrently rendering Nod's piccolo tones into unisex ISBM English. Nod smiled.

Nelly didn't smile at me. Her piccolo tones rang more clear and musical than Nod's. The content was otherwise. "Teacher," her box concurrently said to Kagu, "as you asked, I have set my translator to its *patois*. I reiterate that I disagree with the contact steps you have taken. This animal is primitive. It should not be here. It should not exist." Apparently, only Kagu himself can speak English directly.

Nelly crossed her arms in front of her chest and bobbed her head. Her movements have economy and grace. She stood an inch taller than me, though I felt—primitively—that I could snap her arms as easily as a piece of kindling.

Nod smiled again, almost conspiratorially, at me.

(Nod smiled. Nod smiled—"smiled," I say. And you say, "What can you mean by that— perhaps you see some movement in the muscles of his mask. But how are you to know that

19

is a smile, that it means 'welcome' or 'I am happy to see you' "?

Enough of this question. I can only reply that, as I was with these monkeys, I read intention into facial configuration. You know when a lion is angry, and he is several biological orders away from you—why not expect that monkeys, who are much more closely related to us, will have familiar emotional expressions?)

"YOU HAVE felt real gravity," said Nod's box. "You have felt the awesome force of the primitive world, the planetary swamp, the primeval soup, from which we biologicals all come. Wow!" What his box translated as "wow" was a lip-sucking, slurping sound.

Nod passed by Kagu and brought both paws to my shoulders, his huge brown eyes taking me in. "Litter mate," chirps his box, a shade of enthusiasm cranked into the ISBM modulation. "Little den brother, fellow sentient," he welcomed, sliding his long, spindly arms round me.

Reflexively, I flung his arms aside with a

slight shrug. Though he was half a head taller than I, my movement sent him sailing. He took control of the buffet I gave him, back-flipping, tail swinging, landing easily and bouncing back, laughing. ("Laughing"?—Yes a high-pitched huff-huff-huff in which Kagu discreetly joined, Nelly straight-masked.)

"Come," said Kagu, with a sweep of his palm toward the small enclosure, "let us sit down together."

"No," I said. "Tell me where I am and why I am here. And I must know . . ." But as I said these last words I realized that they might not know my disabilities. I am human. They must have done some damage to my brain in trapping me. Hence I don't know who I am—now— but they might not know this. So I continued, "How long will I be held here?"

This had been going on too long, too clearly, to be a nightmare. So I was in deep psychosis or the human race had finally made its first contact with extraterrestrial intelligences, with creatures who might become our masters or destroyers. Remember Nelly's words: "This animal is primitive. It should not be here." And her final sally, "It should not exist."

"What?" I said, drawing my hand across the sparkling blue sky and the disneyland dream of greenery and rock.

VII _____

"SIR, OUR world is a torus," lisped Kagu, elegantly stretching his long, thin arms and fingers in opposite directions along the azure sweep of the sky. "A doughnut of life about seven miles in outer circumference, five on the inward. We rotate it slowly, sir. Just enough weight to keep your feet on the ground. Hardly enough Coriolis force to register in your inner ear.

"As I told you, our spine tree is Tree-elbow's masterpiece. Cultured from seedlings of seedlings of seedlings fetched up to civilization from

Tau Ceti III several thousand years ago. We call it Vineland, sir. Feel free to explore our world. Except the technology area, of course. A little too dangerous, for now. The metalloids will complain."

Again Kagu's translator spoke "Tau Ceti III," "Tree-elbow," "Coriolis," and "Vineland." Apparently, Kagu's high-pitched lisping English did not include those words. The piccololike sounds that the translator rendered as "Tree-elbow" have a sweet but mournful cadence, while "Tau Ceti III" is a high-pitched discordant hiss.

"Gooddah meetcha, bard," said Nod once more in facsimile English. He held his paw up, palm toward me, but did not extend it to me.

In their furry nakedness I saw no weapons. I could tear all three of them apart with my hands. Did these tall, spindly monkeys control a large artificial satellite?

"What," I asked, "do you plan to do with me?"

Kagu pursed his lips and sucked, brought up his paws in front of him, palms toward me, and then slowly returned them down to his sides. Nelly stared at him, while Nod gave glances, his mug averted.

"Nothing," Kagu finally said. "As civilized creatures, we must, of course, seek to avoid using you in any way or for any purpose. You are free to come and go, to do what you will with yourself and others so inclined. You have but to ask for food and drink. I am sure you will find much of interest to occupy you here in Vineland. You might think of us as a university."

"A university?" I said.

"Yes," replied Kagu, "back the way we came, past the greenery and the rock garden, you find our lecture halls, offices, and laboratories. On further this way you'll find our artists. Of course there are the metalloids, too. The whirgirs and Bootes folk, the few who've taken up residence here. And the flyers, too, of course. But, all in all, it is something like what you'd call a university."

"And what," I asked, "sort of a professor are you?"

"An anthropologist, of course," said Kagu. "As are Nod and Nelly here too. Though Nod has been a trifle lax in his language work. And, as you may have gathered, Nelly doesn't wholly approve of our having you come here."

There was an angry *tsk-tsk* sound from Nelly. Her translator, said, "Teacher, the word is *making*, not *having*, even if it is primitive." Though Nelly spoke the piccolo sounds of the monkey's language, the two operative English words also came from her own throat.

Kagu swung round to her, switched off his translator, and spoke to her in their language. By stance, abrupt hand movement, and sound,

25

I knew his words were angry words. So much for his policy of openness.

I didn't know who I was. But I did know what I was. I was a specimen.

VIII _____

KAGU TOUCHED his translator and turned back to me. "You must understand," he said, now glancing back toward Nelly, "that Nelly here is quite 'artificial.' She is disturbed that we have brought you, beyond gravity, to civilization."

Kagu's words were English except for the harsh piccolo squeal that his translator rendered as "artificial." I wished I knew what that monkey word really meant. For when it came from Kagu's lips, Nelly's lips became a tight line, exposing a millimeter-wide stretch of teeth. And she clenched both her paws into fists.

"It was wrong," said Nelly through her translator, "from the beginning. We should never have . . ."

But I was not then to learn what they should not have done. For from what Kagu called the artist's direction, a score of monkeys swung, soared, and arced toward us through the green profusion of Tree-elbow's masterpiece. Gracefully and exuberantly, forepaw caught branch, body sailed dozens, scores, even hundreds of feet, to where back paws or prehensile tail caught once more, swinging ever forward—the score crisscrossing each other's paths, even pushing and swinging off one another in ad lib harmony. Weighing a half-dozen pounds or less apiece, human-scale bodies in planet-thick air, they were gymnasts in slow motion, taking enormous leaps with effortless, easy poise. I realized that Kagu had done me some courtesy when he walked with me.

Within seconds they settled around us like a modern ballet in which a flurry of dancers, seemingly moving unrelatedly, suddenly coalesce into an orderly tableau. The last one to land unstrapped a wooden box which he reverently laid onto the center of a red, gold-embroidered, ancient-looking silken cloth that the others had placed. Then all but two squatted at the edges of the cloth square.

The two, mugs silvered with age more than

28

Kagu's, walked with slow dignity toward us. The two looked first to Kagu, then to Nod and Nelly, then to me, one of them twitching his nostrils, and then back once more to Kagu.

" 'Hospitality'," said Kagu to them. His eyes shifted back to me and then to them again. "Hospitality," he said again, now in his own English. He reached for their translators and touched both briefly.

"How come you here, grandfathers?" said Kagu.

"We bear the gift," said the grey mugs in unison, piccolo tones and ISBM translator English. "You must join us." The two bowed to Kagu and, with slow elegant come-hither gestures, beckoned him to their cloth table. If you've seen the Leningrad Free-fall Ballet company perform *Talleyrand*, you have half an idea of how graceful they looked.

I couldn't tell whether the invitation included Nod and Nelly—or me.

Now the grey mugs and Kagu settled, cross-legged, in three places around the cloth square. The instant their buttocks touched the emerald grass, what looked like a sun appeared in the blue sky, in the direction they faced—in the artist's direction, where the flyers still wheeled above the waterfall. The sun was reddish and dim enough that you could look at it so long as you didn't stare.

Now the others came to sit, with a little more speed but no less grace than the grey mugs. When their ballet ceased, two spaces were left around the cloth table. I looked at Nod and Nelly, who still stand next to me. Then, somehow, the seated monkeys go through a kaleidoscopic sequence of slight movements, and all in unison murmured the "hospitality" monkey-word, leaving silence and, now, three places around the red-cloth table.

Nod went to one of the places. Nelly stood slackly, then went rigid and started to speak to Kagu. But with her first sound, the sweet, high-pitched, clear "hospitality" cadence came again from the seated monkeys. I walked forward slowly. When in Rome, do! But I did not know which of the two openings to take, so I paused.

Nelly made a slight bow to the table and moved to take one of the places. Apparently, she will condescend to sit with the primitive. Hold your nose, Nelly.

In clumsy fashion, I sat and got my legs crossed. My body felt thick and bloated.

Now one of the grey mugs stretched forward to open the wooden box. Small, ancient, yellowed-ivory, handleless cups went round the table. In order of age, apparently, the grey mug filled the cups with a clear liquid that looked to be water. Then, on tiny rectangular stones, he served each of us two bite-sized, toothpick-

skewered, pieces of meat that look like barbe-
cued pork. No one ate or drank.

The other grey mug read a benediction from
an engraved metal plate. His translator copied
his reverential tone in a lower register. All eyes
turn toward the sky, toward the dim, red sun.

"Remember!" said the grey mug's translator, "Remember! Though countless years have
passed since we grew tails and became civilized, remember! Remember our primitive
origin."

In unison, the monkeys raised their cups. I
quickly raised mine and drank with them. There
were a thousand less elaborate ways to poison
me, and besides, I was thirsty.

"Water," said the grey mug, and as we drink,
I noticed that a tiny planet, blue and cloud-
flecked, circled the sun.

"Earth," said the grey mug. "This time my
hand brought up the toothpicked tidbit with
the rest. The meat was stringy but tasty, fla-
vored with something like soy sauce. After the
first bite, the company relaxed from uniformity.

"Remember," concluded the grey mug, "remember! After the first death there is no other."

The planet disappeared and the sun began
to sink toward the waterfall. Clouds speedily
appeared, the sky became a gorgeous display
of blues, red, and silvers, parsed here and there
by dazzling lightning bolts. I choked as I swal-
lowed the rest of my snack. My eyes watered at

the beauty of the sky. I heard the sweet, melancholic "Tree-elbow" cadence in murmurs from the mouths about me. Nelly stared at me.

Primitive I might be, sister, but I have broken bread with your folks.

IX

TREE-ELBOW'S sunset thundered into silence, the sky in seconds purpling into
darkness. In the twinkling of an eye, the
sky lit up with stars. Bright, steady, myriad
points of white in absolute black. Space.

Real space. A sight beyond the veil, beyond
the gauzy vault of heaven, the reality of endless space beyond gravity—this sea of stars,
each to Earth as large as Earth to his doughnut
world. Except that heaven's vault here was some
sort of clear silicate, cleverly illumed into

33

blue illusion, while Earth's sky was even less substantial, a cheerful mask spun of water vapor and air.

All before was an artifact of satellite technology, the "day" probably produced by a giant, light-altering mirror attached by a beam to the center of the torus. But this must be real. Orion, Great Bear, Sirius. Was Sirius a touch dimmer? Were we near the actual Tau Ceti? Kagu mentioned that the spine tree came originally from Tau Ceti III. Anyhow, by the look of the sky, I couldn't be more than a dozen light-years from Sol.

Now a soft indirect light came up all around us. Monkeys around me stirred. Evidently, the performance was over. I was suddenly conscious that my legs had been crossed together far too long. It's going to hurt more when I stretch them out. Tingles.

By the time I got myself untangled and pummeled my legs into normal operation, the monkey company had departed, murmuring farewells to Kagu, Nod, and Nelly

I said to Kagu, "Is Tau Ceti III your home world? Is that what our meal was in memorial of?"

"The 'hospitality,' " interjected Nod's translator, "is in Tree-elbow's memory, of course. Vigorous last work, that sunset. He must have died when you woke up. And the gift should be

34

consumed before sunset. What did you think we were eating?"

"I thought," I said to him, "that the benediction—all that talk about 'remember'—referred to Tau Ceti, or Tau Ceti III. Wasn't the sun we saw supposed to be Tau Ceti? And that planet Tau Ceti III? In fact, isn't our sun, the real one, outside the satellite, Tau Ceti?"

Nod looked uncomfortable. He turned toward Kagu. Nelly drew together her lips and made a *tsk-tsk* sound.

"No," said Kagu, "the sun we're near is not Tau Ceti. But you are right in thinking that the sun we saw is supposed to represent that star, and the planet is . . . was . . . " Kagu coughed and paused.

"Tell him," said Nelly. Surprisingly, she spoke the English words herself. Her translator issued no sounds. Something about her was hauntingly familiar.

"We did not," said Kagu after a time, "have our precivilized origins on Tau Ceti III, though thousands of years ago we did trade with that world. The 'remember' in the benediction does refer to that time. But of course we met to commemorate Tree-elbow's death. Tree-elbow was the gift."

"Tell him," said Nelly.

"There is no Tau Ceti III," said Kagu. "Now, that is. We *imploded* it."

What about Sol III?

"And so," continued Kagu, "we speak of that time when any of our company dies and so returns to earth and water. We drank Tree-elbow's water and ate his flesh." Kagu did some flowing gesture across his belly, sleek ermine hair against sleek ermine hair, only a flicker of black palm as he twisted his paw. I felt the taste of Tree-elbow and acid in my throat. Ancient meat. My face flushed, the sky and tree closed, the air stilled. Blood rhythmically squirted in the vessels of my temples. Why did they take Tau Ceti III out? Could they—have they—done Earth?

"Oh, litter mate," I heard in ISBM near my ear and felt Nod's paws. "Oh, don't worry, please. I understand that with primitive food processing, such flesh might carry selfish microorganisms, and since you are not unlike us, you might be invaded by such. But there is no chance of this. Tree-elbow's flesh was irradiated, sterilized. Wouldn't carry selfish microorganisms in any case, den brother. Civilization has no place for them. Civilization is too small." He waved his left paw along the outer arc of the torus, along the arch of the deep purple sky. I shook his right paw and arm from my back.

"You tell me," I said, "that I literally ate part of this Tree-elbow's flesh? And drank water extracted from his body?" On top of my stomach's unease, anger flared. My lips formed a straight line.

36

"Oh, tut," said Kagu, his head shaking back and forth, his lips slightly pursed as one who sucked a lemon or one who must explain something simple to someone even more simple. "Tut, sir, you are ... your people are used to conditions on space ships, and on civilized worlds such as our own. If you've been on one of your tiny human ships, you know that you end up drinking water from the bodies of all on board. And if you're on such a ship for any length of time, all the chemicals that make up your fellows will pass through you. Why quibble at a little 'monkey' meat?"

I thought of space bread. Especially if you can't lift anything fancier than one of the old, small Donovan recyclers, you will taste a hint of human origins. Spacers don't talk to earthers about it.

"Tut, sir," said Kagu, "a primitive planet the size of yours is but a larger ship. Eventually, as your Shakespeare suggests, you'll drink the substance of any man, be he old enough. Our civilized confines simply accelerate this process. After the first death, there is no other—for our children revive our substance."

I shook. His glittering eyes pulled me, endlessly I sink into them. These creatures could, and did, "implode" a planet a thousand years before we invented gunpowder. "Soon," he said, as his ancient, slender, furry paws took mine. "Soon you will be part of all of us, for your breath is in the wind. 'Hospitality.'"

X

DRIFTING. DRIFTING. Rolling slowly now, head over heels in the womblike darkness, silence and the distant hush, hush sound of air, in and out, in and out, in and out more slowly. Slowly. Must get . . . slowly, dreamidown, down, down, done.

I sweat. I hear the faint huff-huff of Nelly's breath near my ear. She had come nearer, perhaps because of some noise I made. Her fingers lightly touched my shoulder. I was still not quite awake. Perhaps I had fainted. Perhaps Kagu had touched me with his glass rod again. And what does this dream, or dream-memory, now come a second time, mean?

Some time later, I came fully awake. I was back in the tree-hollow room where I started. The air was cool, the bamboo swayed languorously, the light suggestive of early morning. Nod sprawled on a shelf-nest, forepaws behind his head, legs comfortably akimbo, tail circling hip, its tip lightly gripping a ring a couple of feet above Nod's torso. Nod's eyes widened when I stirred, and he waved at me with his prehensile tail. Useful, such tails, in weightlessness or low weight.

These monkeys really looked like they enjoyed swinging from tree limb to tree limb. Human spacers, especially if they can manage a juvenile start on the gene alterations and hormones, often grow a bioprosthetic prehensile tail. Another thing you didn't talk about, or flash, earthside. I could almost feel how it'd be to have my coccyx snaking out. Of course even a human with bioprosthetic tail couldn't sail like these jokers. They were built for it, long-fingered forepaws to long-fingered back paws, slender frame to supple tail.

"Mornin, bard," said Nod with a grin. "Less make tracks, see the world. You all hab good Z's? Less go." Nod was brushing up on his English.

We both got up. Watch out world. One thing I'm betting on, sister. I'm a spacer. I knew the stuff a spacer should know. And I have the reflexes—in this near weightlessness an earther would be making clumsy bounds, hitting the walls, or tree limbs, or just sailing off, heels over head, into the heavens of this gigantic herbarium. Of course I felt clumsy enough. These slender god-monkeys move much better than any human spacer, tail or no.

It made sense that these monkeys would've picked up their specimen in space. And who would most likely be there but a spacer?

So you said I'm free to travel where I please, Kagu, "except the technology area"—we'll just see about that. "Too dangerous," so you said, but who would it be dangerous for? And what did you mean by "the metalloids will complain?"

I will find out.

XI

VINELAND'S DAWN sky was a delicate tapestry of rose and sand with purple edging. I looked from the artist's end, the distant falls sparkling through soft mists, back across the green sea of bamboo and frond to the brown and white boulders of the rock garden that mark the beginning of the university end. Kagu said that I was in a torus with a seven-mile outer circumference, that being the "ground" toward which a gentle dozen pounds pushes me. The "sky" was just the smaller, inward arc of the doughnut.

41

I believed Kagu. But the sky looked endless, as did the stretch of the land. Imagine an ant in a large display of miniature plants. That's what I was.

Yet, as the sweep of greenery and sky unfolded before me, beauty choked me again. Tree-elbow, you are in my eyes. And in my gut, too, come to think of it.

But there was an exception. A sizable cross section of the doughnut was the "technology area." It separated the university from the arts end, somewhere along the opposite side of the doughnut from where I stood. Got to find out about it.

I saw from the corner of my eyes that Nod stared at me. His huge brown whiteless eyes, pupils the size of dimes, hardly blinked. His lips drew up in a smile as he realized that I see him.

"Want to look round, bard?" Somehow the sound seemed less high-pitched than yesterday. And I almost heard his "bard" as "pard."

I nodded and pointed across the sweep of greenery toward the distant falls. The mist lifted and the sky blued. A lone bat-winged creature soared above the falls. Must be an updraft there. Very little wind needed to support a winged creature in this world. Up the pterodactyls!

"Beat my feet," said Nod as he stepped into the path that Kagu took yesterday. His feet were black-palmed paws. "Lidder brother," he confided, "you felt wild earth 'neath your feet. Not like this place, bard." He was not as good as Kagu at walking. He hopped. Not enough glide to it. Though with effortless tail and forepaw holds, he moved swiftly. Why didn't I have a tail?

Soon we passed the place of last night's cannibal ceremony. It was hard to keep up with him. From time to time, he looked back, saw I'm far behind, then swung up onto a soaring limb to wait for me. So I could increase the push of my legs without sailing high into the air, I used my hands to stabilize my passage, grabbing greenery or limb with one hand after the other. The strength of my grip was too much for the vegetation. I crushed it. My torso swung in a funny rhythm, almost as if my coccyx had indeed become a prehensile tail like Nod's.

The world swung upside down as I lost control and went head over heels, crashing into bamboo, sailing upward along the bent line of the shoots. I knew how a gorilla in a dollhouse feels.

Come to think of it, I was a gorilla—at least I was a tailless, overmuscled brute, in a world of slender, arboreal monkeys. And Nod stared down at me, gently swaying, hanging from one bamboo shoot that my crash missed.

"I trust you haven't hurt yourself?" said his translator. "You left a path like a hippopota-

43

mus." Nod gestured behind me with his paw. I wonder what word *hippopotamus* translated. I had the impression that the translation program tried to be polite. I suspected the discordant whistle at the end of his piccolo tones was the word that got translated so. Sounds dreadful. I didn't like the huff-huff laugh he gave, either.

Nod landed lightly beside me. I shook off the paw he offered. Standing, I could see the falls, though we're in a dip of the path. "Go to falls," I said. "Technology area beyond that?"

"Dass right, bard," says Nod. "Less go."

If this monkey gave me much more of this, I would lose my own capacity for speaking English.

XII _____

FROM WHERE we have come to sit, emerging from greenery, the falls were an endlessly changing tapestry of water framed with the changeless shimmer of several rainbows. *Falls* almost seems too abrupt a word, for the water, made globular by surface tension unchecked by real gravity, undulated languorously over blue-green rocks. There was a hundred-foot drop from the topmost crag to the deep blue pool at bottom. Nod and I sprawled in a grassy sward halfway to the top.

"One of the fourteen stations of falls-looking" his translator called it. The translation had a Japanese flavor about it, but then this world was bonsai.

Bonsai in some respects. Elephantine in others.

A hundred feet above the crest of the falls soared what Kagu called a flyer. Imagine a bat with a fifteen-foot wingspan. Imagine an ebony, fox-mugged monkey as tall as Nod but even more spindly. Imagine his forearms shortening and his forepaws enlarging and webbing. Enlarged and webbed until his absurdly slender and elongated fingers became the struts of his giant but delicate wings. His hands—his wings—were full spread. He floated upon the air, slowly wheeling overhead.

Now he saw us and glided nearer. There was nothing of the raptor in his emerald eyes. More a benign, dreamy indifference. Nod waved at him. Ignoring Nod, he wheeled toward the falls and gently rode the air upward. All children yearn to fly. Remember when Asteroid Sally got her mind tapes transferred from the octopus to a large eagle—and she loved flying so much that she almost decided to stay eagle and not chase Ulgar Fangborn out of her original human body? Most kids, I'm sure, would agree that being an octopus is yucky and being an eagle is grand.

Of course a mind implant like that couldn't

work because an octopus or an eagle simply didn't have enough neurons to absorb the mental software of a human. Even when a nympher sold off his body and had his juvenile mind implanted in a newborn, they have to do it again when he's two or so, just to make sure that the whole memory was transferred. But this emerald-eyed bat overhead, why he looked to have a human-sized brain. What is it like to fly? What is it like to be a bat?

"Ho, there, soil-male Nod," said a more high-pitched ISBM translator voice, "what is this brute thing, no tail and limbs like trunks?"

I turned around and looked up the greenery. Perched on a limb thirty feet over us was a child version of the bat that wheeled above. Her back paws gripped the limb, her wings folded round her, and her emerald eyes twinkled in her fox face.

"Ho, brute," her translator continued, "I feel my talk-box doing your grunts. Like thunder, my body feels it more than my ears."

Now I realized that her translator was also putting out the piccolo tones of the monkey language. My mind had just been canceling out the piccolo stuff. Though her fox mug opened and moved, pink tongue midst white ivories, I could not hear the sounds she—I assume—made. Too high-pitched for my ears. They needed translator boxes in this world quite apart from my presence. Perhaps they all drew on some central computer. It took minimum ten meg-amegabytes of memory to intertranslate two human languages. Those wristwatch-sized trans-lator boxes couldn't be doing the whole job. And besides, would they add neural chips to them all just because I, the brute grunter, turn up?

"Call me human," I grunted upward. Won-der what the translation program will do with that last word?

XIII

"HER NAME," said Nod's translator, "is Drink-The-Sky. She is
daughter of the flyer there above
us. Her father's name is Think-Forever, but Professor Kagu uses a nickname for him, a word
from your language." Nod smiled and huff-
huffed. He stood tall on tip-paw, folded his
arms around himself and then, fingers wide-
spread, flung his arms to opposite ends of the
sky, eyes wide open and canines bared.

"He iss," lisped Nod, trying his own English
once more, "called Count. Good joke, bard?"

"Ho, brute that is named Human. Why are you built so thick? *Was your mother a wrestler?*" Drink-The-Sky hopped, wings slightly unfolded, and landed gently on a limb but ten feet above me. Her slight brown body was covered with hair as delicate as peach fuzz and sleek as an otter's. Her emerald eyes held mine.

"The flyers," said Nod's translator, "dispute our view that intelligent life is monkey in origin. Monkeys who, in primitive planetary life, gave up their tails to walk on the earth with big brains. Monkeys who, once they had slipped the bonds of gravity, naturally reverted to their arboreal life, tailing and handing it from tree to tree. Even your primitive race has already developed bioprosthetic tails for use in weightlessness." Nod's face displays sweet reason itself, but now pain crossed it as Drink-The-Sky's fox mouth issued a sound like a thousand pieces of chalk squeaking across a blackboard.

"Ho, soil-male," her translator continued, "even this brute monster that is named Human sees your view be narrow and silly. Dumb. For what be monkeys but bats who have sacrificed the birthright of the sky? Human, do not settle for a tail. Flight be the natural way of living intelligence, for it be the difference between primitive, planetary life and civilization." Though Drink-The-Sky now flipped upside down, her emerald eyes gleamed at me and I knew she smiled.

"Come fly with me, Human," was what she said. Her mouth warm pink against her small white teeth.

"Thank you, Drink-The-Sky," I said, "but I lack wings."

"Be no problem, Human, for there be sky-harnesses."

"They are," said Nod, "very clumsy affairs. I wouldn't use one. Unnatural. Dangerous. Indeed, whatever the child says, the flyers themselves are highly unnatural, even 'artificial.' "

"Ho, mud-head," said Drink-The-Sky, "your Nelly soil-female be 'artificial.' " We are original—and natural." She released her back-paw holds, eeled easily over while gently falling, and alighted next to Nod. What was it about Nelly? What did 'artificial' really mean?

"Unnatural," said Nod, his back to her, "for flyers did not build or design this world, or any of the countless others through the galaxy. And there are but a dozen of them here and not much more than that in any of the civilized worlds. They are an artistic curiosity we tolerate. A kind of excess of creation."

"Fiddle-faddle, mud-head," said Drink-The-Sky, "tell that to the smart machines in the tech area or to your own shoe-wearer primitives or the metalloid whirgirs, who'd crack your back if the rules didn't restrict everyone's strength to poor monkey-scale. I be plain, mud-head, plain as entropy. All mind strives

51

to rise above earth, beyond gravity, and *we* do so most. Tell me, mud-male, do you dream of burrowing through the ground like worms? No, you dream of flying."

Oh yes, my batling, yes, I dream of flying.

Nod turned to glare at her. With something like a smile, and a high-pitched whinny of joy, Drink-The-Sky shoved herself forward with her back paws, flipped over her folded wings and sailed over the stony edge into the misty gulf of the falls. As her wings flap outward, with a crack, catching the updraft and stopping her fall, I heard her invitation on the breeze, "Come fly with me, Human." She soared upward through rainbows toward the slowly wheeling Think-Forever, her meditative father. The technology area was near.

"You would understand," said Nod, his eyes following them, "why we tolerate the flyers if Think-Forever made music with you—at least that's what the teachers will say. Not that it will happen to you. He made music once with Professor Kagu. And with Tree-elbow, of course."

"I imagine I'd have more chance with Drink-The-Sky." And what was making music?

Nod widened his already huge, brown eyes. "Not her, of course. She won't have the gift for years, if ever." Nod shook his head and pointed up the path that led beyond the falls. "Enough of this. We're late for the meeting. Come on."

"Meeting?" I said to Nod's back as he gamboled up the twisting, fall-side path, tail, all four paws swinging him forward easily and rhythmically. Nod flew in his own way. Anyhow he headed toward the technology area. If I'm a spacer, something there must jog my memory.

Most of the way up in seconds, Nod looked back bright-eyed, framed by velvet moss and tiny, white, bell-shaped flowers. "Come on, just a little get-together," he said, pointedly continuing, clumsily, with just his back paws. "Get a leg on," floated down to me.

I would like to fly in any way at all.

XIV

A T THE highest, fourteenth, falls-watching station, Nod ceremoniously offered me, with a wooden dipper, a drink of faintly bluish water that drained into a stone basin from some fall-side cress and fungi. "For contemplation," said Nod, smiling at my sweating face. I was thirsty but I shook my head. Alice was always running into "drink-me"'s in her Wonderland. Made her high as the sky or low as the ground. She almost drowned in her own tears. And where was the Red Queen in Vineland?

Minutes later, hot and bruised, I entered Nod's little get-together. Nod waved me forward from our hedged path into what looked to be the stage of an amphitheater. Some thirty-odd of his white-bodied, black-faced monkey fellows sprawled here and there in serried, gray-stoned rows that could hold two hundred. Sleek-furred and bright-eyed, they were Nod's age or younger. Perhaps half wore sandals or shoes, and many of these, loincloths. First time I'd seen clothing amongst these monkeys.

Well, it is odd to call them 'loincloths,' but they didn't seem to have buttons, zips, or veljoins. And each one is an individual piece of irregular cloth—like the footwear, each crudely cut, primitive, badly made, individual, non-functional. (Like the moccasins dutifully mal-constructed and insistently worn by Boy Scouts, or puppy-love-tied muslin bracelets, not-to-be-removed-through-all-eternity-or-anyhow-un-til-lover-boy-rockets-off-to-school.)

"Gooddah meetcha, bard," chanted much of the assembly. There was a great deal more of the high-pitched piccolo sounds, for many hadn't turned their translators on. Indeed they were young and sleek-furred, but there was a scruffi-ness about their coats, a studied unkemptness.

Nod slid behind me into middle stage. "Here is Human," he gestured, copying Drink-The-Sky's label. "He is primitive!" I must have a name.

55

The applause was inevitable, and the huff-huffs, though the monkeys without clothing or footwear seemed less enthusiastic.

Two with red loincloths and sandals clattered onto the platform, one the first fat monkey I had seen, the other with a generous splash of brown clay across its chest. Both held their arms out to embrace me. "My savage!" blared the fat one's translator. The other's raucous piccolo was untranslated. Both fumbled at the clay-chested one's wrist, so I was able to step back. A sort of podium separates us.

The scruffy pair raised their paws in a salute. "Speak to us," said their translators in rough unison, "speak to us, man, of savage Earth and planetary weight, of real life. We are revolutionaries too!" Their large brown eyes became larger.

"And we too," echoed several of the audience.

"Down with the grizzle-beards and the mindless metalloids, and all 'artificials'! We have gravity too!" said all, or near all, for a few of the more neatly undressed were silent. "Speech!"

I looked at them, at the garden surround and the endless-seeming blue above. What could I say? That the beauty of your bonsai world is only matched by my feeling of clumsiness at being in it. That I don't know who I am or what threat you are to Earth. (Is there still an Earth?) That you monkeys seem dreamlike and silly, and yet—this I can never say—you snuffed a planet, Tau Ceti III, when our most awesome weapon was the Roman legionary. And yet, and yet, "gravity," *gravitas*, was Latin, the word for what the Romans most prized in a man. Well, I'm heavy. None of you civilized monkeys can dispute that.

Nod regarded me steadily. He must see the sweat on my forehead. I turned and the mass of monkey masks seemed to swell, to engulf my field of vision. They suddenly had faces and each huge, glittering brown eye seemed like a pool into which I will sink. How can they be both absurd and terrifying, silly and in total command? And wasn't that how civilized always seemed to the barbarian?

"Questions?" said Nod.

XV

"**D**IDN'T TREE-CROTCH'S sunset make you vomit?" It was the fat monkey speaking, from where he sprawled at the edge of the stage. "I mean, as a primitive, as one whose low forehead has been refreshed by cooling hurricanes, one who has been bathed by tidal waves. Elbow's work is inauthentic. You see, you know, so ..." His paws pleaded to me.

What was that remark of Kagu's? "So broad-brush," I supplied, wondering whether the computing system would pluck out the same word in monkeyese that Kagu had in mind.

The fat monkey goggled dismissively, though some of the others were respectful. "You joke don't you, man?" continued the fat one, scratching at his loincloth, "broad hose, maybe, or broad geyser—tell us what you feel! Now let some of the really good, the really primitive ... I mean, we could have a real sun. I wish ..." The fat one folded arms across breast, leg over leg, and closed eyes. I couldn't tell whether this disheveled Buddha was male or female. But I do know someone who wanted to run the sunsets.

Nod acknowledged a sandaled but unclothed male questioner, two rows up. "What do you think of old Professor Kagu and his 'artificial'? and what do you think of anthropology?" My tall questioner must be a fellow student of Nod's, for he said "anthropology" in English, though with his lisp it came out *"lan-thwoe-powogy."* What his translator gives as "artificial" is that same raucous piccolo sound. They don't like you, Nelly, any more than I did.

"Professor Kagu," I countered, "speaks my language well. As if he had been studying it a long time. How long have you spied on my civilization?"

"*Primitivity* would be a better word than civilization," sniffed a sober, unsandaled and unclothed older monkey toward the edge of the

59

amphitheater. He stood apart from the rest. "Or *planetarity*, though I doubt this brute has such notions. I suspect our supposedly mindless computer too charitably renders his reflexive belly-rumbling into our weightless tongue. And it is hardly spying to observe, in a scientific spirit, the behavior of primitive animals."

This speech was greeted with huffs, hoots, and shrieks, and the clay-breasted monkey on stage, and some other loinclothed ones, spat in the older monkey's direction. Some of the harsh piccolo-toned calls translated as "graybeard," "metal-lover," "sky-sniffer," "Cato-canter." The spit was something of a slow-moving weapon, for in the near weightlessness, viscous globules sailed, without appreciable arc, toward him.

"In answer to your intended question, brute," he said to me, "better monkeys than these have observed your species for precisely two hundred and sixty of your solar years." He spoke quickly and then exited under the splat of the first globules. No, he was back again, two rows higher. He urinated, directing the stream back toward the clay-chested one and confederates. More shrieks and dodges, the parting shot a comfortable distance from me, and then he was gone again.

Suppose I take him precisely. He was certainly that sort. What on earth happened in 1950 to attract their attention? Or did they just come willy-nilly? We humans have the five wormholes that allow us access to some eight normal (planet-bearing) stars. But these mad monkeys, and their companions, obviously played on a much larger stage.

"You see," said the tall male, "what Nod and the rest of us have to put up with. He, at least, says what Kagu and the graybeards really think. That you're a specimen under the telescope, a planetary wriggler. But we—"

"Want to," joined in Nod in his English, "pee friends, bard."

"So you understand," continued the tall male, "that we share a common bond. Our oppressors are the same. We must join against the graybeards and the metalloids. We must find again the natural in our existence. This blue-veiled dome,"—his paw dismissively stroked the sky—"this plastic artificial sky, must have a stop."

"Yeah," shrieked the fat one, "and to hell with the metalloid whirgirs' demand for strength equal to the brute. Equalization is civility!"

"To hell with the whirgirs. Equalization is civility!" thundered the company. Even the unsandaled and unclothed joined this chant, which sounded, in its original piccolo version, quite unearthly pretty, like something out of Gustav Holst. "To hell with the whirgirs. Equalization is civility!"

I turned to Nod. He bent toward me and explained as the chant went on. "Naturally,"

61

he said through the patriotic din, "the metal-loids are restricted by agreement to our bodily strength and that means the whirgirs, for the Bootes types are no problem and of course the smart machines don't leave the technology sec-tion. Now the whirgirs are complaining about you, because you're stronger than us. They claim they ought to be able to regear to your strength."

"Let me see if I get this straight, Nod. You're saying that all your metalloids—your robots, smart machines, and so on—are restricted in physical power to your scale?"

Nod nodded. "Equalization is civility," he said.

I looked at his long, matchstick arms. I could arm wrestle him down with my little finger. I was to him as a gorilla to a human, more; surely, eight, ten times stronger, though he's an inch taller maybe. Sure, I could probably snap his arm like a stick. So bring on the whirgirs, I can smash them apart like an angry kid with an erector set. Maybe, just maybe, I'm going to save the Earth. Like Asteroid Sally. Like the Trojan Horse. These monkeys were lunatic enough to allow it to happen! But . . .

"But, Nod, partner," I said to him, my hopes at apogee, "if mechanical devices are limited to your strength, how can you, uh, repair stuff, build things, and so on? This is something like a spaceship, right?" They must have picked me up somehow. I mean these monkeys snuffed a planet, right?

"Well," Nod paused, looking at me with the irritation of a parent, asked for the umpteenth time to explain to a nagging child the workings of a modern technology that the parent takes for granted but hardly understands.

(The thought flashed through my mind. *How stupid can this monkey be!* But tell me, can you explain how the tensor director works in wormhole flight? Or how a mind implant really works—oh, sure, you offload the software mind, the memory structures, the opinions and reflex patterns, and so on, out of one brain and then play it into the neurological structure of another—but, damn it, all that's a load of metaphor. I don't understand how it really works and, I bet, neither do you. And we've had both technologies for a hundred years. Hell, I don't really know how you make buttons or weave cloth. And you tell me, specifically, how you make cotton into thread.)

"Well," said Nod, "I guess you could say that our shell and sun mirror, and tech section of course, were built. By big machines and all, long ago in our seedling time, before I was born. But the civilized structure inside here, that grew, you understand, under Tree-elbow's overall direction. We've just never had anything in here stronger than us, and the restricted metalloids, etc. Equalization *is* civility, after all. And of course, I am sure they have very powerful and dumb stationary machines in the technology area."

"You've never been there?" Nod answered me no with the same expression you'd give if someone asked you whether you'd ever visited the sewers.

Have you?

XVI _____

MY EXCHANGE with Nod took just a minute or two, while the "equalization is civility" chant went on. Halfway through, I realized that it changed to harsher squeals of "revolution now! revolution now!" and "red banner! red banner!" And that wasn't all that's changing. The monkeys without sandals or cloths—seven, eight of them— were leaving. The rest came closer to the stage and caroled the new slogans.

The clay-swabbed monkey raised a long

wooden case. The sort of box you'd use to carry a bassoon. He opened it and, holding the box on either end, ceremoniously displayed the rolled flag. The "red banner" chants became more regular and reverential. The brown eyes around me have a dreamy, expectant look.

The fat monkey carefully lifted out the flag, one paw grasping the tip of the pole, the other pulling out the red cloth. He motioned to the tall monkey, who took the grip on the bottom of the pole and waved high the red flag. The tall monkey's face took on a distant look, doubtless revolutionary images flared through his head. He then handed the flag back to the clay-swabbed one, who eagerly gripped it, raising it high. "Red banner!" chorused all.

Now the flag went to the fat one, thence reverentially handed round to several others, one by one in cadence, each paused to hold it with much the same look that the tall monkey had. "Revolution now! Red banner!"

Nod gave the banner the required grip and handed it to me with a wink. What am I committed to now? Not much, I thought. This is not the tennis court oath of the French Revolution, or the signing of the Declaration of Independence in 1776, or Churchill pledging the defense of Britain's beaches, streets, and landing fields in the bleak autumn of 1940, or Getty-Graystoke asking who would step forward to join the final hopeless defense of the Brazoria Republic in 2001.

Hey, now, wait a minute.

The grip of the banner stuck to my hand and I felt a muzzy warmth sailing up my arm from it. *Wow, ee!* I finally pushed it to another monkey. Something has happened to me. The whole amphitheater of monkeys was under an endless pool of water. Everything moved slowly, rainbow bright, sea deep, slow. Revolution, for sure. I am a camera. And it's all so warm and so good but I knew I was out of control and my fingers tingled.

"Red banner! Revolution now!" They swayed and danced. The banner passed on. That's what revolution was for them—a good high. But it was too much for me. The sky slanted, the serried rows wavered, the monkeys ran riot in bodily proportion, hands as large as cathedrals, heads as small as peas. There was something in the banner, something that fed into my hand, like Hamlet's father's ear absorbing poison.

"Red banner!" The words were colors and smells. The monkeys moved in harmony. Nod's eyes rolled large as billiard balls. I saw both of my faces in them. My faces both have large, slack-jawed grins. The colors have almost disappeared into the four pupils. Somehow I think my eyes should be hazel but they are blue, what color there is. Nod's hands grew out of my back. Nod's a lovely guy. They were all

67

lovely guys. "Revolution now," I crooned. I could almost understand their piccolo sounds.

We were all close together, in a half circle around the small stage. All their eyes, their ancient glittering eyes, looked dreamily toward stage center. Smoke and colors rose there, like the genie out of the bottle. I am them. We are us.

"Look, bard," lisped Nod's English near my ear, "we do anthwopowogy. Here come Earth."

XVII _____

THE GENIE smoke became a cloud-
decked blue globe. Small as a grapefruit,
it grew the size of a library globe, and I
recognized the familiar continents. As it grew
to observation balloon size, the lowest part of
it smoothly disappeared into the stage. Some
part of me tensed as it grew large enough to
engulf us, though of course I also knew that it's
a hologrammic display. (Though, if these monkeys get high by holding a banner, who knows
what happens when they conjure up a world

for you. I am not in a position not to find out.)

Beneath the frosting, to the right, swept the sinuous curve of South America, browns and greens against the solid ocean blue, and I could not yet see the Andean backbone, as we wheeled along the Central American hegemony, soared along the white-topped mountains of the Californias, and spun ever westward over the trackless Pacific blue. Earth! My cheeks were wet. I didn't blink.

We passed through Earth's thin upper air rapidly, slowing with the advent of the wispy cirrus clouds. We now barreled below them, clipping along at several thousands of miles an hour, but a thousand feet above the ocean. The sun lay in the purple-gray behind us. Before us came up the low coastline from Hokota to Inubo Zaki. We were following the standard glide path into Narita Spaceport—since the establishment of the Ecological Syndics in Tokyo in 2012, the most famous of earthfalls. I fancied I caught glimpses of Kashima and Katori shrines below.

You understand that beneath the warm, wondrous, giddy feeling, I knew that this had to be holography—and not real-time holography, however advanced beyond what we humans can do. For, however long I savored it subjectively, we have traveled through Earth's upper atmosphere at speeds that would incinerate the slipperiest uriflon in seconds. And, on our lower

70

atmospheric race along the curve of the Pacific, aside from the fictional incineration, the shock wave along our flight path would have made tidal waves and just a tad of noise. But our trip has been as silent and effortless as our velocity impossibly great.

All that is what a quiet voice in the back of my head said. Most of me—my five senses certainly—told me that I was in the final seconds of the Narita glide path. Somehow there had been a transition from the impossible speed of the Earth approach to this. This, this that every neuron in my head told me was the real-time cadence of the standard Narita landing, when your packet boat, gliding in the last few miles from space at subsonic speeds, is just about to touch concrete and sprout parachutes. I must have done this before.

The brief bit of real-time holography flipped into semihologram or flat-screen photography. The single camera itself had become real, presumably planted by my monkey anthropologists. The camera had a point of view. There was no other side to the display we see.

With the real-time glide path, there suddenly came packet glassports, and our visually flat view was that of someone seated in a landing packet boat. A female human hand came up large before me and a male human voice somewhere behind the camera said, "Sally, even an ape knows what to say." Our camera was poised just above the shoulder that bore the hand and in front of us was a chimpanzee.

Through all the warm muzziness—we're lovely monkeys together, right?—penetrated the thought, *I know that female hand,* almost as if it were my own. Following it another thought: *How could a chimpanzee be in a packet boat?*

I had thought that chimpanzees, along with gorillas and orangutans, were wiped out at the beginning of the twenty-first century, the Madness Years, when the Brazoria Republic went down, and apes and computers were banned, before the Syndics of the Concordat of Tokyo made peace, and regular administration, long ago in 2015.

Now the chimpanzee's hand moved quickly, fingers at lips, then upward. "Talk to stars, Sally," boomed the male human voice, "that's what our Earth ape says, or signs, and that's what the Syndics got to say, despite the Man-Firsters. Their next meeting is April 16, 2113, 10:00 T.M.T. A Sunday, that's auspicious, ain't it!? We got a week."

The familiar human hand moved forward to join with the chimpanzee's paw, while from the right, the male human's pudgy hand came into view. "We'll talk to stars," said a familiar human voice.

Around me, though my eyes did not leave the human scene, I heard the huff-huff of monkey applause. I had much to think about. The drug in the banner had me near-hypnotized. My body seemed far away and my eyes drank in the scene projected on the stage. But underneath all this, a small part of my mind was computing, or just crazy and terrified.

I not only didn't know who I was, but I just might have lost two years of my life, or more, because this must be a movie recorded some time ago. I thought it was, somehow, spring of 2111. I'd been in a coma, or whatever deep-freeze these monkeys might have managed, for two years or more. This monkey movie had something to do with me, because that hand and that name, Sally, were familiar. I was so far away from my kind. Why couldn't I draw out that hand, shift the camera, see the face connected to it?

When I first saw the chimpanzee, I thought monkey, I thought that I was seeing some hands/paws-across-space-meeting. The first contact with ETI's. (Aside from me of course, but specimens don't count, do they?)

But the chimp had a low forehead, and arms more muscled than mine. It was just the Earth animal, not one of my huge-headed, spindly monkey-gods.

But my monkeys huff-huffed at it, particularly when human and brute ape joined hands.

Maybe this movie wasn't so much about me as . . . about us?

*   *   *

73

Though I was not conscious that the semi-hologrammic movie had musical accompaniment, something vibrated through me and I knew that the mood was changing.

Suddenly, there was a red-faced, twenty-foot tall man in front of us, booming out, "Natural man, first and last, natural man, first and last!" He was so large I could see the sweat and stubble on his cheeks. Perhaps it was the sheer size, but I had seen so many furred mugs recently that his naked face seemed jarring, unnatural. The Man First motto on his shirt surrounded a slack-jawed, large-fanged caricature of an ape with a red diagonal slash across it. I have seen so many monkeys this human face looks odd.

The man grew small and the chanted din became communal as our camera panned over the scene. There were thousands upon thousands of MF demonstrators, fisted hands raised to the heavens, flowing across a broad meadow, with the Washington monument in the background. The scene swept round so that we saw what the demonstrators saw—several men smashing a robot with sledge hammers. Everyone's seen that shot.

"No artificial intelligence, no mind implants, no off-earthers, no mock humans. Natural man, first and last!"

Now I realized that the demonstrators wore mid-twenty-first-century clothing. Ancient

74

T-necks and lollygobs. This was the infamous worldwide Demonstration of 2056 that very nearly brought down the Syndics. Hundreds of thousands of computers and cyborg monkeys destroyed. Temporary ban on deep space travel and on mind implants. The last real high point of the Man-Firsters, though it was followed by decades in which computers were used, wormhole flight exploration continued, and mind implants performed—but all more or less under wraps, with euphemisms and the like.

The stage was wiped of demonstrators and we were given a simple, dramatic close-up of prison bars. Beyond them one saw greenery and blue sky. Two uniformed Orientals, elderly, spectacled, looked quizzically in on our prison. They made sounds to each other. A high-pitched keen came up, seemingly from where we watched, and a hand—a paw rather—reached up from the bottom of the scene, clenching the bars. We were in a monkey cage and, by the look of that pathetic little white-furred, black-padded paw, a langur monkey cage.

We swept into a fast-paced, snap-framed collage of inside-looking-out cage shots, a world zoo tour, ending with some human-made, black-and-white flat film, surely midtwentieth century, of young chimpanzees, dressed in diapers and garish children's clothing, serving themselves tea, under their zoo attendant's paternal, but mocking, direction. Afterward their keeper shooed them into tiny portable cages. It didn't seem funny.

Now came a close-up of a well-washed pig carcass. I heard gears and it swung left. The camera panned and there was a stream of pig carcasses, hanging from conveyor belt spikes. The sound of a band saw. And somehow the pig carcasses changed to monkeys—macaques, at a guess but not langurs.

The band saw sound spliced us to a spick-and-span laboratory scene. A white-smocked, gauze-masked human surgeon carefully but quickly hemostated the principal vessels of a chimpanzee's brain. Now the action went into fast motion. The brain pulled from its sawed-off skull and ever so rapidly and jerkily inserted in another chimpanzee; both bodies swathed in blindingly white surgical linens. Spliced to a shot of the surgeon, face beaming, pointing to a skull-stitched chimpanzee, eyes wobbling, body chained.

A shiver went down my spine. Oh yes, this must be the original from which the second Frankenstein series derived, you know, the one that started with Dr. Strange Brain in the 2090's. The original, a quite real North American doctor from the final nation state period. Must have been 1970's, something like that, Dr. Fellman, wasn't it? He did brain implants with chimpanzees. Of course they only lasted a week or two, jerking around spastically if they weren't

76

wholly sedated, because brain implants really are impossibly difficult. How can you possibly weave together a million nerve connections, from old body to new brain? I remembered the whole medieval business from some high school course that dealt with mind implants—update your mind tapes and all that good advice. The point the course was making, was that brain implants are cruel, medieval absurdities, while mind implants—reelectrocoding the neurological impedancies in a brain according to the structural pattern of another brain—are reasonably straightforward.

Dr. Fellman beamed over another spastically shivering chimpanzee corpse, and then we spun into another collage. This time it's a real horror show: humans cutting, electrifying, chemically mangling monkeys in experiments from the middle ages, from the 1960's and 1970's. Relief from the horror came with pictures of a primitive spacecraft, lifting from Earth with an incredible waste of reaction mass. Relief was short-lived for the film zooms in to show a visibly terrified ape, festooned with pasted body monitors, being yanked from an incredibly small space capsule.

The sequence almost suggested that humans let apes conquer space first (or pushed them up the chute because they feared to take the risk themselves). As if the brothers Kolokowski, the brothers Wright, or the brothers Montgolfier, would have let an ape, rather than a human, be first at wormhole, heavier-than-air, or balloon flight!

Now a large-scale horror show started. Miniature, hologrammic hydrogen bombs exploded one after another. With each, the blast wave nearly engulfed us before the next explosion. In my drugged state, the wild succession of yellows and reds became beautiful. Around me I heard huff-huffs. The final explosion was ancient, flat black-and-white, the tiny images of huge warships became the toys of an angry child in the blast. This shot was human, this shot I recognized. Eniwetok. It's the one they always show in the history videos—along with "Houston, this is Tranquility Base, the *Eagle* has landed"—to symbolize the highs and lows of the twentieth century, the climax of human warfare and barbarism.

The thought knifed through me. The defiant conservative monkey who left, remember him? He said they'd been studying us for precisely two hundred and sixty years. If it's really 2113, then it must be Eniwetok, way back in 1952, he was talking about. A hydrogen bomb was enough to bring on these planet-imploding "anthwopowogists." Like an aircraft carrier looking in on an island of primitives after seeing an arrow fly.

My head felt hot and balloon big. My body was still paralyzed and I couldn't draw my

78

eyes from the stage. If anything, the banner drug was deepening its effect. Like what you feel when you're trying to shake your way out of a nightmare, struggling to sit up in bed, only to realize that you are dreaming that you are struggling and that you are ever more deeply in the nightmare. All my body shook and struggled to get up, to take my eyes away, and yet I realized my body was absolutely motionless; indeed my outer self was lost in the colors and motions. Get me out of here!

Again a collage. Japanese faces disfigured by flash burns, Arab adolescent corpses draped across barbed wire, Orientals in bamboo cages, human ears threaded like figs on a string, in human black and white the dismal carcasses of shattered cities, a bulldozer pushing impossibly thin corpses under a gateway labeled *Arbeit Macht Frei*. GET ME OUT!

A soft furry hand came from the side of my head and, mercifully, shaded my eyes, bringing the lids down. Both hands took my shoulders and pulled me backward, and up, slowly.

The tall monkey's translator said, "You'll bust his high."

"Spoilsport," said Nod.

"*Oscwiecim?*," said a more distant voice.

The soft hands sprouted arms that held me. In this near weightlessness, I was unwieldy more than heavy. I was a child taken from his crib nightmare. *Pietà*.

79

Then I got a whiff of something astringent. My senses cleared.

Nelly looked down at me. Our eyes held. "They're childish at times. I should have realized that they might pull something like this." Her high-pitched English was as good as Kagu's.

Nelly.

You may have the soul of a schoolmarm. You may be "artificial," whatever that is. But any monkey in a monsoon.

"THERE'S SOMETHING," lisped Nelly, "in your own literature that expresses it, in Plato's *Republic*. Socrates tells the story of a human who knows that there are mutilated human bodies in a street in the town. Some part of his soul wants to look, while the rest of him says no. He grows disgusted with himself and runs to the bodies and looks full on them and says to his eyes, 'Feast!' "

The sky was bright, cloudless blue behind

her mobile, black face, round which sleek, white fur made a halo. Small-nosed, high-browed and high-cheeked, the large, deep, brown eyes took me in but left me myself. They were so large I could see my face in them. The amphitheater of horror-drinkers lay a hedge and two grass paths behind us. I had had a last look at them: bodies slumped but rigid, eyes wide open but dreamy, glued to larger-than-life images of ulcerated chimpanzees used in late twentieth-century cancer research.

"For you," continued her high-pitched yet soft voice, "I think it was like that, especially with the banner slow-feel drug. A part of you fascinated, drawn by the horror, while fascination revolts another part of you. Like a person with vertigo, you are drawn by fascination and held by horror as you look over the edge. But you understand it isn't that way for them. They are children."

"Children?" I said scornfully. "They are full grown. Dangerous as well as silly. They seem to have free run of this Vineland world. And you, you look younger than most of them." This last was true, for Nelly's fur was sleek and white as a baby seal's and her posture had the elegance and spring of a juvenile animal.

"I am . . ." said Nelly quickly, and it was her translator that made it English. "For most of us," she continued in her English, "this would be a compliment and I take it that way. I have

82

my peculiarities. But they are children, or early adolescents, anyhow. For we have a longer period of maturation than you, as you might expect. We allow them what you would think of as much too much freedom. And they are fascinated by violence, perhaps even more than human juveniles. Remember your rebop frizzy holograms, and slimy-feelies."

"Maybe you're right, Nelly," I said, stumbling at her name. There is something in what you say, Nelly. Go ask Alice, who opens her Wonderland by falling down a hole, dropping nearly endlessly, without a trace of fear, and blithely goes on to down a fearsome store of drugs, adjusting her height by taking samples from one or the other. She encounters scores of monsters and mad perversions of language and social convention that would make a Halloween party of psychotics seem a model of reason and harmony.

"Or Asteroid Sally," said Nelly, "when her mind is implanted in an octopus. Your eight-year-olds just love to watch that, again and again, with the rebop meganatched. And even an eight-year-old knows that an optimal human-human mind implant is about the hardest experience to get through for anyone—or any two."

Nelly gave a little huff-huff. In a way there really are two parties to a mind implant. There's the software, what the mind tapes carry, some person's memories, experiences, emotional structure, and all. That's one. The two is the blanked body-and-brain that the psycheticians play the tapes into. But it's a real two because the blanking is never absolutely complete—human bodies aren't ever so many indistinguishable computers, waiting for software. The body has its reasons, as Bruhler said. Oh yes, but there was something odd about Nelly's huff-huff. Not quite a joke, for her. And that name, Sally, was here again.

"Think," said Nelly, "what it would be like to change species with an implant, to have your fingers wriggle out into tentacles, your eyes—do you know, my human, that octopi don't even see, remotely, the shapes we see? Our neat, bilaterally symmetrical shape is just a formless blob to them. Your bare flesh, my hair, are one to them. Whether we crouch or stand might be the big difference."

A drop of water appeared where her eyelids join, shining like dew in a spider's web. In the closer look, her liquid brown eyes scattered into iridescence.

"What am I here for, Nelly?"

"I don't know."

84

TO TAKE a page, if not a whole horror
hologram, from the juveniles, remember
the real reason why the venomous Venusians turned Asteroid Sally into an octopus?
To conceal their invasion plans. Why was Nelly
going into all this implant stuff?

Because, of course, I'd missed the important
question. Sure, Nod and those horror-loving
groundlings like to glaze out, watching their
equivalent of slimy-feelies. Fair enough. But
they weren't watching just any horror holo-

grams, they're watching our human horror show; what we've done to our own AND what we've done to earth animals, just our little local barbecue.

And these "juveniles"—Nod, who's never visited the tech section, and the rest of them—didn't make these holograms. They weren't the real anthropologists. They weren't the ones who implode planets. But Nelly, now, Nelly . . . You don't think I should exist, do you? What about my home world?

"Those movies, the stuff Nod and I watched, why were they made?"

She looked away. Her paw went up, fingers spread. "For all sorts of reasons. Plain curiosity mostly. We are anthropologists. I think Kagu can give you a fuller answer." She looked about, then hesitated. "I think I should go to get him now. He's quite busy. We all are. That's why you got left with Nod. If you could stay here for . . ." She stares at me.

No, now wait a second. I could take her out, easy. But I didn't know what kind of alarm sensors she had on her. She, Kagu, the graybeards—cannibals—they're the kangaroo court, the Red Queen's court, and that horror film was their indictment. I had got to get into the tech section.

"Sounds good to me," I said.

"Kagu will be tied up. It may be some time before he's free. You're free to look around."

"Anywhere?" Was there an edge to my voice?

"Of course." Her eyes looked at me appraisingly. "Why not," she said with a huff-huff, "visit the tech section?"

She launched herself effortlessly into the trees, speeding away, fore and back paws and tail effortlessly slinging her along, a litheness dancing through greenery into the distance. Oh yes, I wanted to fly.

Her last words echoed. "We'll have no problem meeting up again. Your translator gives your coordinates."

My eyes held the small, featureless wristwatch affair, nestling in the sparse hair of my forearm.

I pulled it off, wondering at the ease with which it loosened. They must be very sure of me. Let us see what the savage can do.

XX _____

AHEAD OF me rose a wall. Out of all the gracefully irregular greenery—the soaring bamboo, the olive and purple maple, the low-nesting ferns—it loomed unfashionably flat and philistinely geometric. And loom it certainly did, all the way to heaven. They'd colored the upper reaches a changeable blue, so that until you're this close, it seemed to be more of the sky; indeed it still faded into it way up top. It was the wall at the end of the world, of the mad greenhouse monkey world.

I needed to remind myself. I was inside a doughnut that rotated very slowly. Just enough artificial gravity so that things didn't go floating off in all directions. The green-swaddled ground that stretched behind me was the inside of the outer surface of the doughnut. The blue sky was an illusion created in the half mile of air that reached from me to the inside of the inside surface of the doughnut. The miles of air that curved off, imperceptibly, behind me until they reached the tech section from the other end. Only here was the illusion imperfect.

The contrast unnerved. I felt like walking up and actually touching the wall. I had just come out of a sheltered path, naturally the trees and creepers reached high here, to preserve the garden world illusion. I sweated. Took me something like an hour to walk here, mostly along a winding path, and just now picking through the masking foliage. It would take one of those monkeys a fourth that time or less, elegantly gliding from tree to tree.

I saw no doors, no entryways of any kind. Still, this wall must reach from one side of the doughnut to the other—nearly half a mile. I thought I could see the juncture of inner shell and wall to my left. So right was where I'll go. How the hell, Nelly, was I supposed to visit the tech section?

A few minutes and several creepers later, I saw a sort of answer. Instinctively, I ducked into shade. Through the greenery ahead, two monkeys glided toward the wall, sweeping forward in efficient leaps of twenty feet or so, branch to branch, some sixty feet from the ground. They both wore blue harnesses around their midsections. With the end of the trees, they both sailed forward toward the wall. And now I saw an opening, a long rampart in fact, that my eyes had failed to pick up, it being blue against blue, and some seventy feet up. The monkeys disappeared from my view.

Soon I could look straight up at the rampart. No stairs, the wall below it as smooth as ever. I looked enviously up at the tree holds they had used. A good hundred feet from the last one before you reached the rampart. Even if I was one of those human spacers who go the bioprosthetic route to get a prehensile tail, I wouldn't have a chance of making that sort of leap.

Not just that I couldn't leap that far, but you got to consider landing, too. One of the nastiest lessons weightlessness or near weightlessness has is that inertia remains unchanged. If you go sailing into a solid wall at ten miles an hour, *it doesn't matter whether you're earthweight or weightless, you hit the wall just as hard either way.* Earthlings always have several really nasty smashes before they get the hang of it—which is why in anything close to weightlessness you always strapped them down and padded everything in sight.

I jumped straight up. Sailed up twenty-five feet or so. At the apex, I tried to grab onto the wall, but the surface was smooth as silk. I have to be careful landing.

Third jump I went all out. Close, but still twenty feet short. And the lunge had cost me control. I fell back, with increasing speed, into the bush. A good springy handhold helped break the fall, and all I suffered was a couple of scratches plus the strain on the hand that took the hold. Falling forty feet held real danger even if you weighed only twenty pounds. For efficiency and cost, any artificial space structure uses thin, oxygen-rich air. That means a lot less air friction on falling bodies. So if you fell a long way—a couple hundred feet—your velocity would really build up, and you were in serious trouble. I mean like your leg-bones-spearing-up-through-your-gut type trouble.

My face burned. Sure I could visit the tech section, Nelly. Yeah, if I could fly.

Come to think of it, maybe I could do just that. Maybe, given the confusion of this place, I could do just that.

Almost before I knew what I was doing, my feet moved into a good moon-walker glide, back to the falls. Drink-The-Sky, you got yourself a student.

91

XXI

"HO, BRUTE that is named Human, have you lost your furry fellow soil-male?"

I whirled as the sweet high-pitched ISBM voice came up behind me. She had flown the updraft from down the falls while I looked past the top of the falls toward the arts end, where her father, Count Think-Forever, still soared, his fox face dreaming. She settled elegantly on a slim branch, which she caught with the tiny, slender fingers of her back paws, while a finger, halfway along the leading edge of her partly folded right wing, lightly grasped another limb that extends just above her weasel-lean, otter-sleek body and brightly smiling, green-eyed, fox face.

"Nod," I replied, "is watching movies."

"Ugh, be smelly nervous, watch that stuff."

"Scary, certainly."

"Hah, mud-men. Someday my father make music with them, huh? Then they know fear, huh? They should fly. Even you, whose mother was a wrestler, and whose thunder talk makes my translator box thump, even you should fly."

"Teach me."

Out of her fox mug, her emerald eyes grew thrice human size. "Oh, Human, yes. I will."

The vast cave she showed me, having led me past the fourteenth falls-looking station and over a lichen-decked, tiny stone bridge down the other side of the falls, was well, though softly, lit. Two adult-sized flyers hung down, asleep, in the inmost and dimmest reach.

"I thought, pardon me, that your kind liked darkness." Drink-The-Sky hovered a few feet above me.

"We do, Human, like the splendor of the night sky. Good flying then. Few mud-men about and the stars are real. Sometimes the day be too bright, for our eyes be much sharper than mud-men's. But you need some light to see."

Her small fox mouth moved and I caught glimpses of her tiny white teeth, against her ruddy tongue, but I heard no sound except for the ISBM English from her translator.

"Perhaps you can use your voice echoes to navigate in total darkness?"

Drink-The-Sky looked back from where she opened a compartment that blended into the gentle, stony curves of the cave wave. "Human, you might do as well, with your rumblings. The same for both of us if we have to go down in darkness absolute or if we were blind. Flyers use voice to talk. And to 'make music,' but I cannot do that at my age.

"Of course," she eyed me and gave a whistle just at the limit of hearing, which her translator rendered as a monkey huff-huff, "of course, on some planets our distant ancestors—tiny, insect-eaters—use sound. But that no good for even a flyer a fifth my size. We are the eagles of the night, Human."

From the compartment she pulled a black fabric structure with one wing finger, closing the compartment with the other. "Here," she swung the structure toward me, "put your harness on. Fits furry mud-men. Should fit you."

Looked like a collection of folding umbrellas. But Drink-The-Sky nodded toward two holes that were obviously intended to take legs. I pulled the gear on, sort of like pulling on the rubber overalls that fly-fishers wear.

Much more of the gear involved the arm holds. With a little help from Drink-The-Sky, I got my hands all the way in. It's then that something remarkable happened, something like, but much grander than, the sudden way in which automatic umbrellas spring from limp, bunched cloth into large, rigid, airy hemispheres. I felt electric tingling all through my arms, and my fingers seemed to stretch out into large, webbed wings. This is an enormously sophisticated piece of cybernetic engineering, and a joy forever.

Truly marvelous feeling. I raised my wings, stretched them to full length on either side of me. Call me Dracula!

A S I spread out my wings to their full extent, my fingers feeling as if they have suddenly been stretched out six feet into a fan—a lot of knuckle-cracking, that—I teetered and flopped backward, settling helplessly on my back.

"Here be one fallen angel," said her cheerful, high-pitched voice. Her emerald eyes gleamed down at me, her tiny hand-feet clenched my waist. "The first rule be to fall forward, Human." Her right wing folded in toward my face and the pinion finger hooked my collar. She stepped, leaned back gently, drawing me up slowly. Somehow, she timed it right and I moved my feet up under me and stood. I swayed a little, but her cool eyes held me straight.

"Come," she said, waving toward a structure much like a gymnast's horse but with grips at only one end. It rose up from the floor of the cave.

"You know how to swim in water, Human?"

"Yes." Somehow, I knew I could, and both in Earth gravity and low weight. It was like that with my skills—they just came out but I didn't know how I learned them—breaststroke, crawl, golliwog. I felt less desperation about knowing who I was. Enough to be human now.

"This be like swimming underwater. You draw your wing-hands forward squeezed, and then cup the air on the way back." She looked up at me and I understood how well she walked with her pigmy hand-feet, and how much she put up with me to do so.

"Bend over it," she said. "Now straighten. Be still." And so I was while she eased me into position on the horse with her two middle pinion fingers. Her breath came in puffs. I knew that I should hang onto the grips with my feet, and I managed, belly on the horse and my instep hooked underneath the grips.

"Yes, that be it, furless mud-man."

I had to arch my neck to see her dark, peach-fuzzed, fox face, framed by the high collar of her folded wings.

"Cup, feel air like water, pull back and let fling. Fold, limp-wrist, draw forward. Gentle! Now cup. Feel the air and pull.

"Pull, Human, there be hope."

We were at it for perhaps an hour before Drink-The-Sky helped me off the horse and gestured toward the sky framed by the cave entrance, her delicate right wing-hand gracefully unfolding to full six-foot length.

By now I realized that the harness had a safety-conscious mind of its own, one that gave the most gracious interpretation of my fumbles, superwaldoing all the way. Though the real power came from my arms, my fingers not only felt six feet long, they were in real control of that stretch of fan skin. You know those funny neurological drawings where they draw parts of the human body in proportion to the quantity of brain-nerve connections—where the fingers are larger than the arms and legs combined? It was like that. And my feet almost felt cupped, and tiny.

I stumbled and scuttled behind Drink-The-Sky toward the entrance. The sky drew me. Must be satellite midafternoon by the bright look of the sky.

"Go," said a voice near my ear. A few more feet of a stony shelf. Then the trackless stretch of air, flowing down the watery flashes of the falls, sailing over the greenery and moss-decked stony surfaces that swaddled the falls, soaring into blue as far as my eyes could reach.

"Can you see the end of the sky?" I asked her.

"A torus, dear mud-man, has no end. Let me show. Go!"

With a gulp, I scuttled forward over the edge. Let slip the bonds of earth! The phrase was appropriate, for the rotation of the whole torus drew me toward the inside of its outer surface. I go, Drink-The-Sky, I go.

First, just the float, the glide, the bright rainbows of the falls rising up like pillows below me, as I gently sailed down the course of the river. Bonsai filigrees of tree and shrub, rock and gravel, spray out left and right toward the horizon.

Above my left shoulder Drink-The-Sky wheeled in. As her bright eyes caught mine, she flicked her face left.

I dropped my left wing, pulled with my right, and now the falls flexed below me. I zoomed over the "fourteen station" with Drink-The-Sky, in easy harmony, holding over my shoulder.

Yes, again, a brief glance, and her muzzle nodded upward, a suggestive forward shrug of her pinion shoulders.

Up! Cup and pull, cup and pull, cup and pull. The firm full muscle pull exhilarated. I was much stronger than her, but after several beats, she still flew easily above my shoulder. I caught her eyes.

"Fly, mud-man, fly!"

It took me a second to realize that I hadn't actually heard these words. I read them into her tiny muzzle.

Fly we did. Low weight much more than compensated for our massive size and the thin air. Drink-The-Sky guided us into an updraft and we rode upward.

The falls sparkled behind us. Several hundred feet below us curved greenery and garden, endless intricacies of greens, purples, tans, and browns, delicately punctuated by flower beds rainbowing through reds, yellows, and blues, all faintly sectioned by the curving paths, whose snow-white gravel showed here and there. Ahead of us, from where Kagu first woke me, rose the great growth of Tree-elbow's masterpiece, a tree—the tree—whose sprouts soared small everywhere behind us, a tree that here rose and spread, with what planet-gravity would make airy and delicate impossibility, several thousand feet. My eyes teared, while some cunning inner voice speculated that this mass of wood compensated for the tech section.

"Climb, mud-man, climb!"

But it was not the one tree alone that compensated, for I now saw beyond it the outrage-

100

ously slender, ivory towers and quaint copper-green domes of Kagu and Nelly's university.

The updraft that whistled up past us died in the faint, cloudy wisps. The air was moist and fresh. The inner surface of the doughnut must end some couple hundred feet above us. But I still could nót see it in the endless bright blue illusion created by the satellite's mirror and some nearby sun.

Cup and pull. Cup and pull. Cup and pull!

Drink-The-Sky's brown-black wings stretched out scores of feet below, faint cloud fingers streaming back from her pinions.

Cup and pull. Cup and pull. Cup and pull!

The air breezed my sweating arms. The blue darkened precipitously into steely purple and I glimpsed stars along the horizon, the mirror's brightness above. As if your spaceship shot through the hundreds of miles from the lower atmosphere to the black ionosphere in seconds. And with the same air, oddly, still skidding by your cheeks.

Suddenly, out of illusion, appeared the silicon vault of heaven. I was within a few feet of hitting it when my harness suddenly went numb and rigid. My breath went out with a whoosh and I saw the steam. I wheeled slowly downward, the blue heavens reappeared, and the harness once more was in my control.

"Be careful, Human, or the harness will be careful for you." These words from her transla-

101

tor were the first I had actually heard from her in flight. The green eyes and muzzle formed a smile when I looked up over my shoulder. Now I had that illusion of hearing again. "Tsk, tsk, mud-man. Follow me down!"

Naturally, if they let idiots like Nod use these harnesses, there must be protective overrides. Not, from what I'd gathered, that the monkeys much enjoyed using them. Doubtless because it reminded them that swinging from tree to tree was an inferior way to get around. Yes, surely Asteroid Sally was right to be intoxicated by the life she led with her mind implanted into an eagle. Of course with planetary gravity to work against, nothing with a brain large enough to maintain human consciousness could actually fly. You get a few mild violations of reality in children's stories. But here I lived the dream.

Correction. We lived the dream.

I banked and swooped, my harness guiding my wings into a partial fold, and I dropped after her, the air whistling past. In seconds we have dropped several hundred feet. When I saw Drink-The-Sky pull out of her dive below me, a hundred feet above one of the great high-soaring limbs of Tree-elbow's masterpiece, I could feel my harness easing my wings outward.

A tall, elderly monkey, taking his afternoon walk along the several-hundred-foot limb, his tail protectively trailing behind, smiled up at us, his ancient brown eyes glittering gaily. I followed Drink-The-Sky into a sharp, wheeling dive, and now we slipped below the limb, coming out the same side but now below, as we began. The monkey waved. Drink-The-Sky looped and flourished her wings at him. That particular maneuver looked quite beyond me, or my harness.

Suddenly, I felt tired. But more than that, the monkey reminded me of the point of learning to fly. I turned back toward the falls, where we began. I must be as near, or nearer, to the other end of the tech section, which must be somewhere beyond the far side of the university. But back this way I'd seen the entrance. An entrance, at least, for those who monkey leap—or who fly.

XXIII

A S I soared over the last high-reaching bamboo stand before the tech section, the reddening sun arced a few degrees above the horizon to my left. The rampart hoved up. Scores of feet long but only some eight feet, top to bottom. A tight fit, that, the way I lifted up my wings and stalled to land. Manageable, maybe.

Apparently deserted.

I had left Drink-The-Sky with the excuse that I should solo. She seemed skeptical but unconcerned. "Monkey business," was her parting sally. I do not think the flyers worry much about monkey matters. She waggled her wings, peeled off and plummeted down over the falls, far faster than I'd seen her fly before, pulling out just above the rainbowed mist of the fall's bottom, and slalomed away through treetops. "You fly like elephant," had been her assessment of my capacities.

I glimpsed a lit corridor leading off from the back of the rampart. Also apparently deserted. The stony rampart doubled into my eyes. Close now. Careful. Up wings.

Whap! I floated, a few feet from the rampart, something holding me up, the same thing that arrested my descent. Felt—over my shoulder, it was—a balloon. Damn. Another part of the protective system. Too much risk the monkey will muck up the glide in, so the system pops the balloon parachute. Either that or it's designed to keep the wearer away from forbidden areas like the tech section. So let's find out.

No wonder Nod and his bunch don't get themselves hurt. This whole world was baby-proofed.

As I arced away from the rampart, the balloon fizzled, retracting into a bubble on the back of my harness. I folded up my wings into a slow stall and landed on the grass below the seamless tech section wall.

Teetering this way and that, I struggled off the harness from my arms. The legs were easy.

105

Though the world seemed less exciting as the black umbrella collection lay lifeless on the grass.

I grabbed the bubble that held the balloon. It had the look of a safety device, something that dutiful inspectors check on a periodic basis. Here goes. I grabbed the edge and yanked, then confidently tore. Off it goes. Maybe that'll short the rest of the system. So then I'll daub my fingers with superglue and sticky-paw my way up. As good Drink-The-Sky said, "Climb."

I wriggled back into the harness. The shades of night were falling, or rather, being drawn down, by one of Tree-elbow's successors. The heavenly sequence was surprisingly pacific, considering the last night's operatic display. Gorgeous blues and roses gave way to purples and reds.

I stretched out my wings seven feet left and right, taking the feel of the sky. The feel was all there, system apparently intact except for safety override. Eagle of the night, rise!

The draw was the same and I pulled up. Cup and pull, cup and pull. I hoped they're all watching the sunset.

The corridor was a cone of brightness as I wove in from the darkness. I stalled fine, my feet sailing in just over the rampart, my wings folding enough to slide under the roof, spread enough to slow the landing speed to a walk. Good for night's black agent.

The rampart area and the corridor that led in, past several doors, some hundred feet or so before it curved out of view, were quite empty. All silence. I stripped off the flight harness. Stash it at the furthest end of the rampart, can't hide it more than that. Better yet, I'd carry it. Doesn't weigh much.

As I stole down the corridor I felt a sense of comfort or security or whatever from the sharp, regular angles, the orderly rectangles of doors, the precise right angles with which wall and floor and ceiling joined. I could not read the curlicues that scrolled out a few inches above the handles to the doors, but I knew that they labeled the rooms beyond them. I decided to follow the corridor rather than to try the hatch handles.

I fancied my eyes picked up the very slightest of curves that came with long structural lines in the well and economically designed ship. If you ask me, even octopi are going to build spaceships a lot like ours, though who knows about their gardens. I've got to find a boat. By space and monkey logic, it must be built so I can con it. I loved to fly with you, Drink-The-Sky, but now I needed wings of fire and the big, black sky, cold as Kelvin absolute and wide as the Milky Way.

Okay, yeah, the logic is to go where the artificial gravity leads, because that's the outside, where the boats will be and where they can be launched.

Hatches to the right of me, hatches to the left of me, narrower and higher than human ones. Now came something simple and efficient, a pole descending, and ascending, into cylindrical openings in floor and ceiling. A great way to go where the mild artificial gravity would push you, and not hard to go up against it, though likely they had elevators, or whatever, for that. Let's explore.

XXIV

I SLID DOWN two levels.

The broader corridor I floored out on stretched several hundred feet. Disappointingly, though, nothing showed that looked like portholes, air locks, or packet boats. Probably I hadn't got to the outer shell.

I stood stock-still. Some distant monkey figure appeared at the far end of the corridor and then busily went on into what might be an elevator. I breathed.

Still, down that way must be where to look, at least if I stay on this level.

Halfway to where the monkey disappeared, hoved up some humorous relief to the sleek, modern, philistine efficiency of the tech section. A copper statue, a kind of medieval caricature of a computer robot. Spherical body with nineteenth-century riveting, sticklike arms and legs, feet with ridiculous spats; pop-eyed, basketball head, again with those ridiculous rivets. What a crazy place this was.

In fact, I now saw that it was not a caricature of an electronic computer robot. Obviously one wouldn't think of electricity that long ago—or whatever long ago it was for monkey history.

It was a caricature of a clockwork man. The artist had made that obvious enough, for next to the statue's feet lay a large key of the sort one might use to wind up an antique mechanical clock. The absurdity of the copper clock man was heightened by the engraved labels next to the three holes for "winding" the mechanism. The antique letters spelled out THINKING, SPEAKING, and MOVING. Appropriately, the MOVING windup hole was much more heavily constructed than the other two.

I now saw that there was a smaller key, presumably for "speech" and "thought," most of it covered by the large "motion" key. I supposed one could interpret this as a satirical comment on the dominance of action over speech and contemplation. Though, that would be a little dumb because, in fact, a real computer that employed clockwork mechanism would have to be the size of a house and every cranny of it filled with clockwork more precise than most Swiss watches. That's why Charles Babbage, who tried to build one in the 1830's, failed, though the British Government, at the plea of the Duke of Wellington, bankrolled him sumptuously. Here I was running through the old high school Computer ABC's course.

Even remembered that hologrammic textbook cover showing the outside of that huge, mad, playhouse construction, "Frankenstein's Head," just outside of Tokyo, that Prodo did in the 2090's in honor of Babbage and Alan Turing. Man-Firster protests to the Ecological Syndics about that. No one likes modern art. Little copperman here was quaint and inoffensively tiny by comparison. Though who knew what offended these monkeys.

I had so many memories. I could *see* that textbook cover, but somehow, not the hand that held it. Why couldn't I remember who I was?

Beyond the copper statue to the left, there's what looked to be the entrance to a theater or large lecture hall—or an art gallery, in keeping with the copper statue. Might as well take a look. Everyone's apparently at dinner. Which

111

reminded me that Tree-elbow was the last thing I had to eat. Hunger and disgust mixed in my stomach. I felt a little light-headed but I could wait. Just wish I could find the launch deck.

"I wouldn't go in there if I were you." With none of the monkey backwash, the words were ISBM English. I stepped back and whipped my head around. I couldn't see the speaker unless it's the statue or a remote. The statue didn't move.

It could be just a warning device that tripped when anyone tried to enter, an electric eye or sound detector or whatever. I stepped forward again.

"I wouldn't go in there if I were you." Exactly the same line, so it could be automatic.

But now wait just a second. What was it doing delivering prohibitions in English? Damn, was this bonsai beehive that good? Did the system see me everywhere? Biological identification, tailless monkey anonymous, under care of Professor Kagu and Researcher Nelly, please return to keepers. Say it isn't so. Please.

Oh, but now wait another second. I was being very stupid indeed. What was copper kettle doing with slogans engraved on it in English, huh? What were the roman alphabetic letters, THINKING, supposed to mean to monkey folk, huh?

I turned directly to the copper clockwork, to

its basketball head and goggle eyes. Okay, you, a human can gape at a kettle. You want to fight?

The black pop eyes were empty. I gestured toward the entrance.

"I wouldn't go in there if I were you."

I couldn't see any movement in the goggle eyes or copper face. Was the sound from there?

"Why not?" said I.

"Hah, got your attention, my silliness. So, is your prejudice against copper or just against metal? You, human, at least should acknowledge me."

"I thought you were an art work."

"I am, I am. No need to disparage me." The copperman added some suitable whirring and ticktock sounds, and winked one eye.

"You're some sort of computer-robot."

"That, too, dear animal." One absurdly quaint mechanical hand went up and dipped a copper homburg hat toward me. The movement was jerky, like a caricature of early machinery. Both eyes winked. Interrupted by a stray ticktock, the mechanical voice went on. "You know the expression, 'Oh, what a masterwork is man!' You certainly should, for your race made up that conceited phrase. Well, if you can be a work of art, whether or not a masterpiece, *and* a computer-robot, I don't see why you wouldn't allow as how I can be both too."

"I'm not a computer-robot."

113

Both eyes popped. "Don't disparage yourself. Certainly you are. You compute—minimally, at least—you figured out that I was talking, eventually anyhow, and I'm sure you know what two plus two equals. And, rather obviously, you move yourself about. Therefore, you are a robot." Copperman raised both hands, palms toward me. "Since you compute and you robot, I conclude you are, most certainly, a computer-robot."

"Computer-robots are made out of metal. A lot of copper, by the look of you. I am flesh and blood."

"Piffle. Monkey-logic. Hydrocarbon chauvinism." The copper head nodded at me. The eyes popped. "Silly, anyhow. I'd like to see what would happen if we took the metal out of you. Without your iron your blood would die, without magnesium and manganese your brain would short out. 'A lot of copper'—pure piffle. You need copper, for your animal metabolism to function. I just wear copper, pretty though it may be, 'tis just my plume. The ticktocks are just sound effects." Again the homburg dipped, with flourishes.

"In short," copperman continued, "my chips are rare earths framed in silicon. No metal in *my* brain. But there's plenty in yours, human."

"Look, copperman," I said, "you are an electronic mechanism. You may be strong and you may compute quickly, but you were designed,

114

built, and programmed by Kagu and his race. You are a robot. You are not a free being. I am."

After a moment of silence, there came a multitude of ticktocks and metal hiccups, the button eyes winking erratically. The copperman raised his sticklike arm and shook it. The motion was slow and jerky, and hardly frightening.

"There, see," copperman said, "weak as a monkey. Weaker. Last year, when I took my sabbatical on Tau Ceti V, I was built like a bulldozer. Then I could lift ten of you in gravity twice that of your water-soaked home planet. I could've picked your limbs off with my smallest appendage. *Grr*. But here . . ."

Copperman's arms went up, cranky and slow, his eyes popped again, and he made something like the monkey's huff-huff laugh sound. "You know the rules here. Us Bootes folk are limited to the pathetic strength of an average monkey. 'Equalization is civility,' hah! I'm already running down. What a cost there is for authenticity and true art." And copperman did seem to be running down. His hands remained held up in protest and his eyes no longer popped or winked. His voice, however, ran on.

"You mark my words. Bootes folk like me don't mind being mammal weak, being as how we're artists, but you monkeys had better watch out for the whirgirs, they're chauvinist, technocratic brutes and they're spoiling for a

115

fight. 'Equalization is civility,' hah! Depends on whose rheostat's cranked down.

"And it's perfect piffle about the monkeys designing or building me. Far too difficult for them. I designed, built, and programmed me. True, my father/mother, a self-made creature much like me, did put together my original megamicrocircuitry some two hundred years ago. But father/mother did it freely and creatively and consciously, not, as you were made, in an animal spasm of unconscious physical reflex, with your parents having no more idea of what specific model they were creating than do a pair of frogs. I've been modifying the original model in a million ways since, something quite beyond the capacity of you biologicals, who are as set in your ways as concrete. Just yesterday I put together my copperman body, a play upon your own literature. 'Free being,' hah! I'm freer than you'll ever be, human. Just try to change your body sometime. Change age for youth, one height or sex for another, the triumph of freedom and intelligence over biological destiny. I do it weekly, when I'm in the moooowd."

"Copperman," I said, unable to resist a rhetorical counter jab, "what you say is true, I'm sure. But the fact remains that your body has run down, while I can move as always. So you are not free."

I turned again to the entrance.

"I woooouldn't goow . . ." The clockwork voice wound down and out behind me.

I went.

THE ILLUMINATION was theatrical, the walls black to better set off the display. My heart pounded and my throat thickened. Human!

Stiff, set up on a white circle like a clothier's mannequin or animals in a natural history museum. Stuffed, by sun. Heavy build, low brow, bright eyes, weathered face, heavy jaw, scraggy beard. Oh no, not stuffed. Neanderthal.

Actually, the brow wasn't really low, or the jaw and build all that heavy—just low and heavy compared to Kagu, Nelly, Nod, and company. I'd been seeing too many monkeys. But it still wasn't stuffed. Cro-Magnon, or whatever, there hadn't been anything like this running around on Earth for tens of thousands of years. Now I saw that he held a crudely shaped stone in his right hand. A few bone tools displayed in a raised case next to him. Now I saw, to his left, his mate, with suckling infant. My face was warm. I felt very far from Earth, and very close.

I was in a gallery, not a theater. And not an art gallery.

The next oval down to the left sported an ape much like the one I had seen at the start of Nod's show. A chimpanzee probed a rotten tree with a delicate stick with one hand, while holding an infant casually with the other. The infant chimpanzee's small-jawed, high-foreheaded face was startlingly human.

Beyond the chimpanzee squatted a much less human-looking ape, probably a reconstruction of prosimian, the human-ape ancestor, whose skull Caroline Leakey discovered in the 2050's. Beyond prosimian, predictably I guess, a real Earth-style, small-brained langur. Still further left, a tiny, prehensile-tailed spider monkey. I wondered if they had a bat beyond that. Would Drink-The-Sky care?

Enough for the distant past. I turned right.

An Egyptian scribe busy at his tablet, the

119

giant charioted pharaoh scything through tiny Nubians on the wall behind him. Images of his gods—Nubis the baboon, Horus the hawk, Bastet the catwoman—on an altar shelf.

A well-gowned Japanese samurai family, the prepubescent boy's two swords diminutively echoing those of his fierce father. Laid out on the reed matting in front of them, a scroll painting of a whiskered monkey brushing Chinese characters, overlooked by another, who smokes a pipe. Through a sliding door at the back of the samurai's house, one saw nearly naked peasants industriously distribute sprouts amid the rice paddies.

In an eighteenth-century dining room, wigged and silk-stockinged gentlemen bowed to slim-waisted, vast-bustled ladies, while black servants (slaves?) bore in platters of quail and pheasant. On the wall, I saw a quaintly colored world map and prints of steam-powered mine machines, horse-drawn coaches, and wooden sailing ships issuing broadsides.

A mid-twenty-first-century fresh room, woman in an old-fashioned tolong, man with slimy-feelie goggles and gloves. On the wall, the old MF plastilogo, an impossibly well-muscled man with one foot stomping a gorilla, the other crushing a robot.

The gallery ended with a sharp turn. Let's see what the future holds.

My face was burning, everything seems bright,

my heart was pounding. Before me, real as my hand, set up on a white circle—a cataloguer's display sign a yard to the right—stood a MAC3 space suit, standard for the professional asteroid miner. Zaldar tool kit, with Belt modifications, heavy-duty power pack, heinlein-waldo gloves, double-skin, Melrick gold-film visors, the complete bit. Real, real as my hand.

My spine tingled, my head felt like it's bursting. I knew the suit. I knew the suit.

And now the lollipopper. Somehow it's a total surprise. Somehow I'd known it had to happen.

Me. Standing in the display circle just beyond the suit. Me. My body. The face seemed a little strange, but I'd only seen my face a couple of times since I woke up, once reflected in Nelly's eyes. But then, your face always seems strange, and I'd been seeing nothing but monkeys lately. Monkeys and bats. Bats. But the hands and legs. Oh yes. Me.

And then me (it, I, my statue body) began to speak. My head bigger than a balloon and bursting. The statue body said, "I am . . ." The deck reached up for me. My legs rubber. Down I go. Into the umbrella pile. Out.

XXVI

DRIFTING. DRIFTING. Rolling slowly now, head over heels in the womblike darkness, silence and the distant hush, hush sound of air, in and out, in and out, in and out more slowly. Slowly. Must get ... Slowly, dreamidown, down, down, done.

An arm along my right side, a hand gently cupped my hip. My head bent, slumped and suppliant, against some warm chest. I heard soft, even breathing over my nape and neck. A gentle, rocking motion soothed. Soft fur and warm. The slow, even beat of a heart. I floated, more than half asleep. Safe.

Out of a great distance, I heard a soft, high-pitched crooning. A lullaby. The words seemed familiar and wonderfully comforting. Yet I couldn't quite sort them out. As if it were something like "Rock-a-bye-baby" but sung in a sweet Yorkshire lilt. I floated, my mind full of the crooning.

Almost imperceptibly, my sense of the lullaby changed. It was the monkey language. Yet it was soft and infinitely comforting for all that. I could understand the words. I understood monkey. Almost. Sort of. Who cared? Wonder. Wonder. Wonderful. Wonder full. Wonder fills.

Nelly. Of course it was Nelly. I knew all along.

Yes. There's something funny about that dream, that so often repeated dream. I moved so slowly, turning head over heel. And I didn't seem to be wearing that MAC3 suit. Maybe if I could just fully grasp that scene, that last scene before I lose two years and my identity, I could get it all back. Somehow it didn't matter. Nelly.

I opened my eyes.

Thin, delicate, small black nose. High, straight, coal-black forehead, and high narrow cheekbones, small, sharp chin, all haloed by impossibly white and sleek fur. The thin, aristocratic lips still moved, the soft, high-pitched croon still held, the echo of a trance. The eyes, the large brown eyes, were like pools into which I might endlessly sink. She was so close that I did not quite focus. Her face shimmered across the horizons of my eyes.

A long pause, then a smile slipped across her lips.

"You do seem to have an extraordinary way of opening doors, my friend. When I suggested that you might look into the tech section I had no idea you'd learn to fly in order to do so." Her lips pursed, but a grin curled up the edges and she shook her head from side to side. "You could, simply, have asked one of the doors to open."

"Doors?" My lips felt caked. My blue utility overall was gone.

"Any place along the tech section wall, and there's a door within twenty feet. The ship computer will hear you unless you whisper."

"I didn't see any doors." Where was my flight harness?

"Naturally. The wall isn't supposed to look like a wall; there's an attempt to preserve the illusion of the limitless garden. What you used for entry is a sun deck. Not supposed to be used for entry, though some freer spirits flip in that way."

"What's the operating word for the doors?"

"*Open* will do quite nicely, my friend. The

ship computer speaks English—along with a couple thousand more plausible languages—so it would understand you. The translator you managed to lose is just an extension of it."

She gave me a wink. A rather elegant and distinctive wink. "You aren't trying to lose me too, are you?" She stretched back along the line of the padded platform. No one in this world wore clothes.

Her hands cupped her knees. The backs of her long, lean fingers were lightly frosted with white fur, the elegant thin nails, platinum-gray. As she turned one hand, I saw that the palm and fingers were black. I was close enough to see the swirls of her fingerprints and the larger lines that a fortune-teller would read. And what would he read there for you, Nelly?

"Why do they call you 'artificial,' Nelly?"

She gave a little jerk when I said the word. She looked at me for a long time.

"Well," she said, "you certainly can ask questions." She got up and beckoned. "I think you are hungry. And I think I shall need some time to tell you about myself. If I can. Come."

We were in something like the chamber in which I first met this world, a seamless, graciously curved, accident of Tree-elbow's one tree. Nelly led me out to a small niche amidst the soaring growth of limb and creeper. She laid out a table.

Soon we crosslegged ourselves on either side

of the low wooden bench that would, in the dazzling complexity of its grain, rival the Milky Way. Steaming cups of clear red herb tea. A rough, grainy, brown bread. Nelly tore off a piece for herself and me, and then, measuring my eyes, gave me her piece and took mine. I took a bite of the bread but held her eyes. Then I reached for her cup of tea, but deliberately brought my hand back to my own. She smiled. We both sipped. Astringent but fruity.

And there was fruit. Firm, crisp red-skinned fruit, shaped like bananas but the texture and taste of apples. Large pink grapes that delighted the tongue with the tart sweetness of pomegranates. I took more of the bread. I was quite hungry. I drained my cup.

There was a pitcher of clear water. I remembered Professor Kagu's stern lecture to the effect that everything we ingest was at some time part of our ancestors. I poured some water in my cup and raised it to Nelly. "Tree-elbow," I said with a smile.

Nelly raised her cup to mine, gravely. "My human," she said, " 'hospitality'!"

"Tell me," I said.

She carefully set her drained cup down. "I am not what I seem," she said. Her high-pitched lisping English squeezed my heart.

    "**I**MAGINE A male of my race to be born on a multipurpose artificial world much larger than this one. This would be, oh, roughly, ninety of your years ago.

"Oh yes, that is a weary long time ago, even for us. I could give you the precise number of years and the Earth star-chart name of the satellite's sun, and the man's name for that matter, if I said them in my own language. The translator on my wrist would give the equivalents." Nelly shut her translator off, undoing

127

it from her wrist. "Even the ship won't listen in on this. We're alone.

"Our race discovered long ago what yours found out a few decades back; that while you can, for all the danger of rejection, transfer the software from one body to another, you cannot avoid essential mental senility. Though our minds, on average, may last a little longer than yours, they cannot have much more than a hundred years of actual, lived experience, no matter how many bodies are called in to serve. So our scientists have long concentrated on preserving the good health of our bodies. There are no 'spares' because you can't grow a healthy, functioning body without producing a mind at the same time.

"Oh yes, yes. Just like on your Earth now, there was a time when a very wealthy person could buy a young body, buy it from a nympher who could use much of the cash to convince a pregnant woman to allow the nympher's mind tapes to be played into her baby's brain. But our race sickened of the practice and so mind implants became forbidden except in extraordinarily rare cases. Cases in which a blanked body became available through an accident in which the brain suffered enough to destroy memory and personal identity, while the gross neurological system remained essentially intact, so another mind could be implanted. But, with our steady advances in medicine and safety, such an accident has become very rare indeed. Even so, our race came to feel that such blanked bodies could not possibly be sold, so even if one became available, it would not likely be used."

Nelly didn't look at me. Her words were slow and careful. Now she turned toward me. Her look intense, pleading.

"The urge to live on is as strong among us as it is with you. It is not so implacable with the whirgirs and the Bootes folk. And the separation between one person and another is not so clear with them. It must be curiously relaxed to be a robot. But with us the urge is so strong that what makes death and aging bearable is that we know it happens to us all, without exception. After many a summer dies the monkey, too.

"So imagine this male of my race, born ninety-odd years ago. Imagine him once an intense young man, a historian who reveled in our galaxy-crossing peoples, and sure he had more to say about this spread.

"And indeed, so he did. He produced several studies that were read by historians and are still occasionally referred to in footnotes in some of the standard texts. He also courted a mate of great beauty, wit, and family. Their relationship, which is rather more formal than your marriage, produced no young for many years. His 'wife' created 'song-poems'—I call them that, for there is no exact equivalent in your culture—and as our male grew older, these song-poems became much more famous than his historical work. Many are thought to be an expression of love for him. The ship's computer translates the usual name for them as 'Leave-Takings.' Not bad, though I like plain 'Fare-wells.' Of course, no expression in your language can translate . . ."

Nelly's lips voiced a melodious, fluty phrase that had sorrow and eternity in it. From the language of these creatures who coursed the stars before pharoahs built pyramids. Leave-Takings.

"In middle life, both go on an unusual pil-grimage. They take ship alone on a yearlong trip beneath two ancient and famous galactic-central stars—not wormhole flight, but slower-than-light drive. Capella and a red giant, I don't know your English name. There is some small danger to the trip, for they are truly isolated. No radio signal or ship can go much faster then they, for they are outside the gossamer of wormholes that allows communication and travel through the galaxy. But they see this isolation as attractive. They are in good health and their ship is a type well-known for reliability.

"But now the unexpected. It becomes clear that the woman is pregnant. Quite extraordi-nary after several decades together. They don't have the fuel to turn back, to reverse their

130

near-light speed, and any appeal for help will have to travel at little less than their own sublight speed. At first it doesn't seem threatening. What could be more natural than childbirth, and it seems most likely that the flight will be completed before the birth. But the pregnancy was further advanced than they thought. And the birth came early.

"She was very old to bear. Though they both put on a great optimism, both were frightened when the contractions came. The mother died, her white body fur sopped with blood, and a month later the ship reached civilized space with a newborn and a worn-out, terribly shaken middle-aged man."

Nelly had kept her eyes from me while talking. Her hand clasped her tea cup and she looked cold—shivering—though it was warm for me.

"So the man felt tragic loss. But he cannot give way, for the child must be raised. They lived in one of the vast satellite worlds of Capella, a major center of the galaxy. She was a brilliant and loving girl. In her early teens she became a word-master, and she began to work on her mother's song-poems."

Nelly looked in my eyes. I realized that her hand held mine. Somehow it seemed natural. Her hand was dry and the fur on the back tickled. The small pink mouth must open again over the firm black chin.

131

"Her work is thought to make her mother's song-poems rise from brilliant to profound and the work is celebrated today. 'Leave-Takings,' is still the favored name.

"But there was more tragedy. Her elderly father began to suffer from a degeneracy disease, perhaps a cancer bred by radiation exposure during the long lone run. A number of unsuccessful measures were taken. Death sat near him. But then his daughter's body was discovered. She had taken a drug that reduced the oxygen flow to her brain just enough to blank out her personality and memories.

"In a letter, she offers her body so that her father's mind may have a decade or two more of life, implanted in her body."

Nelly's grip has become almost painful. She made a conscious effort to loosen it. I could not look in her eyes.

"It is more than an offer. She pleads, demands. She points out that since she—her mind—is dead, all that can survive of her is her body. That is her memorial, and he must occupy it. He must ensure that the revised song-poems, her lifework, are properly published and distributed. He must preserve 'Leave-Takings' for her."

Nelly had stopped speaking. I heard her breath go out in a long sigh. I knew I must look in her eyes now. There were no tears. The empty

132

eyes stared beyond me. Then she lowered them and they gripped my eyes full.

"I am that man, of course. I have his memories." After a pause she lowered her eyes and went on.

"Oh yes, he realized, as he read that long, at times incoherent, letter, that his daughter had long nurtured an unhealthy passion for him. And he realized that he should have understood this long ago and taken steps to help her out of it. And he realized that he had been blind to this for jealous reasons, because he wanted her love. And he realized that her pleas were, in their own crazy way, reasonable, given the irrevocability of her act. For the song-poems did need care that he couldn't give them in his last ill days. And there were other things that needed tidying up."

Her eyes came up again and held mine.

"Yes, I—he, whatever—was painfully aware that he might simply, desperately, care only about avoiding death. That is another reason our culture does not approve of implants. What might a sister ask or give her brother; what might a mother ask or give her offspring; and what of lovers? No, we do not permit such questions. But he faced them.

"Of course he felt horror at the way she destroyed her mind, at her puzzling, loving and hating, act. But who knows what really drives

133

one? What he held on to was the thought that if he thought of her act as loving, he must accept the offer of that love. Though he has not told anyone of his reasons until this day. He could never say these things to one of his race."

Nelly slowly filled her lungs and let her breath out. She blinked a little.

"The implant was performed, and performed with conscientious skill, though I think all concerned felt that it was a last favor to one who now would be beyond the pale, one who should have died. So mind and body made a kind of peace with each other. The revised song-poems were tastefully published and distributed. And I sought to put as much distance as I might between myself and our cosmopolitan culture, and all who had known either father, mother, or daughter. So I came several years ago to a small research installation in an obscure part of the galaxy. So I came to bury myself in the study of a primitive and alien animal and its world."

There was a little strangled huff-huff. "So," and now Nelly smiled slightly, "I came to know Earth."

Here was a time when I could use the rude strength I own in this strange world. Without thought, my hands went to her shoulders and I lifted her easily over the low eating table. She was my height but her lean, fragile frame folded,

134

knees against breast, and I held her, this ancient juvenile, as a mother might her child—indeed as she held me—and now the shuddering sobs started, so many years in coming. She cried as we.

AND THERE was more she does as we.
In my two days with the monkeys, I
had grown used to their undress. Anyhow, human spacers, and I'm pretty sure I'm
one, often go naked or near naked unless they're
working on a passenger liner—particularly on
small ships, cleaning clothes was not a simple,
or cheap, problem. So the old joke was, "He
put his pants on, so I knew he was thinking of
only one thing."

I held Nelly as she sobbed and jerked, simply

feeling those sobs and jerks, muffling them, patting, comforting, making the wordless sounds that you made. Suddenly I realized that I was kissing her, my full heavy lips against her thin. And with that realization, another. My penis had come erect between her buttocks and my belly.

I think I felt in her sudden stillness that she has had the same realization. The sobs and jerks were over. Her lips left mine and briefly returned and left more finally. I eased my rude organ away.

We pulled our bodies apart. I thought I saw a flash of flushness between her legs as she turned. Our eyes catch, embarrassed, then knowing each to be embarrassed. And then the grin, the grin that flesh-made mind is heir to.

"You do," I said, "have an extraordinary way of opening doors."

XXIX

AN ALIEN cough rent our privacy.

"Your servant, my dears," said that familiar antique voice, "you do seem to be enjoying yourselves." Professor Kagu stood just outside the grove. His eyes rather obviously patroled the heavens. But even in profile I could see his smile. It occurred to me that one obvious advantage of habitual nudity—certainly for the female—was that you couldn't be caught with your clothes off.

"But," continued the urbane professor, "I fear

that I need your help. And my need is immediate and urgent. The whirgirs have demanded a meeting." Kagu bowed to us, as if to excuse his haste. Nelly stood and stepped toward him.

Kagu beckoned me. "A meeting about you, my itinerant friend, about you and yours. I am dreadfully sorry, particularly to throw you in with such short notice, but there it is. Our hand is forced by events. You will have to speak for your people, human. For Earth and its satellite worlds and colonies. For all your people."

Kagu looked at me directly and carefully. "For all your people. Think what that includes."

All? What could that hint mean, Kagu? Hope they don't play the film Nod showed. What am I to excuse or explain? Hitler? Hiroshima? Verdun? Auschwitz? Slavery? Houston? Adam? All humanity?

Nelly turned and held me with her eyes. What seemed a long time ago she had said of me, "This animal is primitive." Had she meant to *protect* me—or the entire human race—from something?

"Come," said Kagu. I put on my overall and picked up the flight harness that lay beneath it.

Nelly took my free hand and gripped it firmly. "Come," she said.

I went.

They moved forward in the "swimming gait." They set out slowly, out of politeness to me.

But unconsciously, as they moved on, they used hand and tail holds and soon glided forward faster than was comfortable for me. I still felt uncomfortable about lacking a tail. Nod had called me something the computer translated, doubtless politely, as "hippopotamus." With Drink-The-Sky it was "elephant." What comparison will strike the whirgir's fancy?

The verdant, careless fairy greenery stopped. We trotted through a half acre of formal gardens, extravagantly sculptured rainbows of flowers, hedge, and gravel that made Versailles look like someone's backyard garden. Then, as if to compensate, a rock garden, on a much greater scale than Kyoto's Ryoangi, but with the same severity and simplicity, and tantalizing sense of order. Ryoangi was seven large rocks set like islands in a sea of wave-grooved gravel the size of a tennis court. This, much larger, garden, what world did it represent?

A quarter mile later, I breathless and they unaffected, we moved among the high, delicate towers of the university. A turn down some sparkling marble steps and we stood in an amphitheater like the one near the falls, but with a different and more serious population.

There were two dozen monkeys. Perhaps half were graybeards, the rest Kagu's age or a little younger by the look of them. Nod was there and waved enthusiastically, but there were only two more of the juveniles, both sitting with

140

him. One I remembered as the tall, "revolutionary" anthropology student, though he lacked sandals. No evidence of the fat, loinclothed would-be sunset artist or his clay-caked comrade.

The most striking, and numerous, were undoubtedly the whirgirs. Surprisingly humanoid, or monkeyoid, they wouldn't be allowed on Earth itself. The Man-Firsters were still powerful enough to prevent that.

Also surprisingly, after the copperman, they all looked much the same. Their surface looked like stainless steel, though here and there at joints there's plastic and the like. They appeared even leaner and more delicate than the monkeys. I nearly laughed to see one reach up with its silvery tail to take a paper from another.

Kagu, Nelly, and I walked to our appointed place, a box of three seats, each an arm's length from an ornate golden handle. We hardly seated ourselves when the one with the paper addressed me. It had a microphone mouth and two camera-lens eyes. The anthropomorphism did not extend to nostrils.

"Earthling, we are most happy to finally have an opportunity to talk to you." I heard its remarks from a small speaker on the back of the seat in front of me, a foot from the golden handle. I was unsure whether its face speaker was actually issuing sound—certainly I couldn't hear it. But the other whirgirs did, in some way, for they leaned forward in unison and gave me a nod.

"We whirgirs, of course, are not anthropologists. We have little interest in primitive worlds. True, the monkeys also live in civilized worlds. Indeed, they simply cannot stand up to planetary gravity, while we can, with suitable adjustments. We simply recognize planets as what they are, savage, dirty, dangerous environments, entitled to privacy and unsuitable for civilized machinery. But some monkeys nurture an unhealthy interest in savagery, romanticizing a distant, primitive past to the degree that they cannot actually experience it." The other whirgirs collectively nodded through this, agreeing.

"But, Earthling, we have heard enough to make us concerned about your people, especially about your racial types and conflicts. Are you immersed in *inwhirgirality*?"

It took me a second to realize that the translator came up with that last word from "whirgir" as we derived "inhumanity" from "human."

"It is true," I said, "that, until fairly recent times, various human races and nationalities have puffed up themselves with feelings of superiority. Light-skinned peoples, particularly, mistreated and disparaged darker-skinned ones. But this has virtually disappeared today. Of course there are always minor lapses, but overall, there's a recognition that all humans are equal, that all have an equal right to basic

142

freedoms and opportunities." I couldn't believe I was getting so preachy. Can that ancient phrase "life, liberty, and pursuit of happiness," be far behind? I ought to pull the golden handle and start a triumphal organ fanfare. Still, we hadn't done so badly the last hundred years. And even the incredible savagery of the twentieth century saw the real beginnings of the end of extreme racial and sexual inequality.

The whirgir spokesthing shook its head. "As I understand you," it said, "you speak about the equality of members of the particular tailless-monkey species to which you belong. Now it is true that members of your species are not equal in the precision manner of us whirgirs. True equality is mechanical." Measured applause from the other whirgirs at that. "But in the messy, primitive manner of animals, of monkeys and apes, of course members of your subspecies would be equal. What else would they be—all indistinguishably gross, anthropoid, and vermin-infested." Four score of implacably expressionless camera-lenses took me in. What's the spokesthing getting at?

"When I speak of your 'racial types and conflicts,' I naturally mean things like your subspecies' exploitation and extermination of—what are they? I have the terms here—*chimpanzees*, *gorillas*, and other fellow tailless apes." Serried ranks of camera-lens eyes stared.

"Of course this animality is not of real concern to whirgirs, and naturally, it is the monkeys who must judge this behavior. But I speak of something much more serious. Namely, the relationship between your subspecies and the metalloid Earthlings. Tell me, human, what do you think of—I have the words here—Earthling *computers* and *robots*? Tell us." Forty metal faces made the same reproachful nod and then stared anew.

"Tell us. We have learned that long before you had thought of building metalloids, the word 'robot' meant just 'slave' in one of your languages. Tell us."

Had the Man-Firsters really, finally done us in? Nelly grasped my hand.

THOUGHTS FLASHED through my mind, some dredged up from Computer ABC's. Wait! I could see a hand holding that textbook cover, a hand looking childlike and unblemished compared with now, but then— but I can't afford to think about that now. Alan Turing first argued in 1950 that if a computer can *pass* as a human cognitively and psychologically, then that computer thinks, believes, desires, feels, and so on. Surely, Turing wrote, it isn't fair to ask the computer to have our

145

skin, or our skin color, or our sex, or a human-like body?

Cunning argument, that. Because what showed that blacks and women have equal rights with white males was that blacks and women could pass as white males cognitively and psychologically. Skin color and sex shouldn't count against you; but if color and sex didn't count against you, why should metal skin or microchips? Remember how copperman sassed me? Am I the slave-master Simon Legree to these whirgirs? What was the phrase, "Equality is . . ."?

"Well, human, what of Earthling computers and robots?"

"Spokesthing, whirgirs," I said, "long before humans built . . . ah, long before multipurpose robots and computers *appeared* on Earth, writers and scientists of my species speculated about the possibility of intelligent computer-robots. True, some chauvinist individuals—lately we call them Man-Firsters—have been reluctant to recognize that metalloids can think and feel, and hence have rights. Indeed, they have blocked the creation of robots with a primate body structure. But," here goes, "long before the Man-Firsters, one of our scientists, Alan Turing, proposed, in effect, that 'Civility is Equality,' just a stylistic variation of a familiar slogan here." If cameras could glare, they were glaring. I better finish quickly. "He argued that if a computer-robot can speak civilly about a mul-

146

titude of subjects just as well as a human, then the computer-robot is the equal of the human."

"We," said the whirgir spokesthing, "are gratified to learn that at least some members of your subspecies are rational." Simultaneously, the ranks of whirgirs raised their stainless steel right arms in salute.

"I ask you, human," and now it pointed to a screen which had helpfully risen from the proscenium, "what that is." On the screen was a diagrammatic image of a standard industrial robot transporter. Squat, square, four-wheeled, with a heavy-duty forklift, periscope sensor unit, feelies skirting the sides; you see them around factory yards and warehouses.

"It's an Earth robot," I replied. "Moves heavy materials about." Played the block-slab game with builders.

"Can it climb trees?" was the spokesthing's next sally. Bit of a stopper, that. Could you image a transporter climbing a tree?

"No," I answered, "of course it can't."

"Can it manage the navigational controls of a ship?"

"No."

"Can it operate a keyboard?"

"No." After my reply, it waved once more to the screen.

"What is this?" On the screen, a tenth generation Cray-Ada sig-parallel-pross mainframe, googol-byte, multitheater fluid hologrammic display, the whole schmear.

"It's one of our most powerful computers."

"Can it move objects with precision from one place to another?"

"No, it doesn't move objects around at all. It doesn't move. It's a computer."

"Does either the Earth robot or computer in any way resemble this, which does with ease all the things I've mentioned?" On the scene, inevitably I suppose, was displayed a whirgir. The question being rhetorical, the spokesthing simply continued. "Fortunately, your Man-Firsters have some sense. Doubtless they will see that whirgirs are the natural perfection of nature, of biological evolution."

Fat chance of that. But let it blither on. I caught a sliver of a smile from Nelly and our eyes held. What it must be to experience so fully the split of mind and body, to have remembered an aging male body and awake having taken on a young, female one—and such a taboo one. Nelly was unnatural, outcast, self-doubting.

"Yes, the whirgir is simply the most tried and true biological form, the primate monkey, infinitely enhanced through its realization in enduring metal. Is it not obvious that the fleshy primate should eventually achieve perfection in incorruptible, undying metal? What else is the obvious trend of evolution? Give a primate enough time and intelligence, and what else will he make but metal creations? What else do primates make tools and statues of? How do they immortalize their baby's shoes? We are the eternalization of biological destiny."

She knew, more than this whirgir ever could, that our vaunted personal identity was just an accidental confluence of thoughts and feelings, and a physical mechanism, whether flesh or metal. She could love me—miracle, that, if true—because she was beyond the cozy confidence of race. I was like her because I had no secure sense of identity. I knew various things, without knowing how I came to know. I had a body but don't know what it's been through. No mythic sense of a necessary synthesis, a history, a self. Nelly. Oh, Nelly. Eyes are enough.

"Human, we are content that Earthlings now pose no threat to the settled order of evolution." Forty slim stainless steel right hands turned their thumbs up. "I have only one final thing to ask you to do. You see that golden handle in front of you?"

Yes, sure, I'd been looking at it for the last ten minutes. All metal, but indented in the manner that once might have been metal wire compressing leather in ridges around the tine of a sword, the handle projected half a foot from a squat cylinder. "Yes, I see it."

"Could the robot or computer we projected pull such a handle?"

Are wheels hands?, forklifts fingers? Can a Cray-Ada dance? Was there shade on the sun?

"No."

"Would you please pull up on that handle? Hard!"

Brute strength I got, and frustrated enough to use it. I grasped the handle with my right hand and pull. It gave an inch easily, another with some difficulty. The more I lifted, the harder the resistance. With a grunt, I put my legs into the lift, and gave it my best.

After an inch or so more, it suddenly gave. I went sailing several feet back and into the air. Luckily, Nelly and Kagu grabbed on as I went past, so I sank back without causing much trouble except to the startled graybeard on whose lap I momentarily landed. In my right hand was a heavy-duty key or odd-shaped screwdriver.

There was a palpable silence. The whirgirs, in unison with their spokesthing, slowly swept their camera eyes from one end of the monkey audience to the other, as if to say "Hah! did you see that?" For me, the scolding effect was lost when their heads continued through a complete circle.

"Gentle monkey-persons," said the spokesthing, with grave emphasis, "what we have suspected has now been amply demonstrated. Professor Kagu, Honored Seniors, I must admit that when we called this meeting, on the eve of contact, we had comparatively little concern that Earth presented illicit pretentions to whirgirality. What is now, most clearly, far more serious is the presence of this Earth monkey in Vineland." Now the spokesthing looked up and down the ranks of whirgirs. His hand came up like a conductor's baton.

"Equality is civility!" The delivery was apparently simultaneous, every whirgir chanting —or whatever they were doing—as one. The chant was repeated several times, while the slim metal bodies shimmer and wriggle emphatically. At last they quieted. The spokesthing resumed.

"The situation is even more shocking than we thought. We had thought to demonstrate that the human could exert several times the pull that is now the limit amongst us. You must recognize that we used the sort of restraint device that keeps air lock keys from children. We recalibrated the device by a factor of more than five so that we could test the obviously much greater strength of the Earth monkey. We are shocked that he could pull the key out completely. Surely, you must concede that with such a monkey in Vineland, the strength limits for whirgirs must be increased fivefold or more. Or, the alternative is clear."

Nelly was on her feet. " 'Hospitality,' " she called. I heard the English from my translator. But just as clearly I heard the sweet, high-pitched cadence. She looked straight toward

151

the whirgirs, unwavering. Kagu turned, and looked over the graybeards and younger monkeys. " 'Hospitality,' " he called, and the high-pitched monkey murmur spread and echoed. " 'Hospitality.' "

Nod and the tall anthropology student popped up and down, the one pulling the other down before himself jumping. I think they were screaming "primitivity," anyhow it's some other motto.

When the piccolo tones died down, Kagu addressed the whirgirs. "We must recognize this Earthling as a guest, a stranger. This is first contact." The whirgirs shimmered and wriggled but this time with a sound like gears grinding. "And," continued the implacable professor, "he must be accorded the respect appropriate to first contact. Tit for tat. He is not one of us but an independent envoy."

The whirgirs suddenly stopped moving. Their spokesthing raised both metallic paws to heaven, the first gesture uncopied by its fellows. "I simply don't know," said the spokesthing, "how we can continue in face of such intransigence. Strike! Forty-eight hour switch-off strike!" It swung its face from side to side, while the other whirgirs renewed their wriggling. "Comrades, do we have strike?"

"Strike, strike, strike," echoed from my speaker as the whirgirs raised their stainless steel right arms and fists. "Dismantling to the biological garbage-grinders! Forty-eight hour switch-off!"

The entire whirgir assembly, protagonist and chorus, gave a final shake and then, in quick rhythm like a fall of dominoes, sequentially collapsed back into utter immobility. Silence ensued.

Kagu slowly shook his head. "They're always doing that."

I put a key with a golden handle in my over-all pocket.

"THEY'RE ALWAYS doing that," repeated Kagu. "And straight away my shower will start spurting hot water viciously, and the recycling unit will throw the garbage back." He winked at me good humoredly. "I'm absolutely sure they plan these breakdowns." He shrugged his shoulders, bringing his hands together, black palms up.

"Remember," huff-huffed Nelly, "when they had a switch-off two years ago, protesting pickup of the *Baleen Blanco* wreckage so close to Earth orbit? Nod and some others burgled the pharmacy, took megadoses of 'swarmy feel-right,' climbed the great tree, and spent the whole night and the next day there hooting. They said they wanted to embrace the heavens."

An Earth ship? Wreckage? Must have sent in a boat to get it because anything large as this doughnut would have been detected anywhere near the solar system.

"I bet we would have, too," said Nod's translator, "if gaga old Tree-elbow had only let the tree grow another fifty feet." Nod and his tall buddy had come up from their seats. "Of course," Nod continued, "I wouldn't do anything like that now."

"You certainly won't, my boy" said a nearby graybeard's translator, his parallel piccolo tones sizzling, "for we have fixed the pharmacy, so that it's secure even without the whirgir attendant."

"Professor Kagu," I said, following up Nelly's hint, "you mentioned first contact, but you picked up the wreckage of an Earth ship two years ago. What's going on?"

Kagu looked uneasy and hesitant. Nelly stared at him.

"We've," said Kagu, "been extremely busy these two days since you awoke. Not your fault, of course, and you deserve a lot more attention." He smiled. "Though I do understand you have been undertaking your own education, ganging about the heavens and the like. But I expect it's time we do something for you ourselves. Perhaps you would care to look at the record of our intervention? Not a pretty picture and after our mistake we had to make the best of some bad choices. You should see the way they scorched us in the *Primitivity Review*. Much nastier than the whirgirs." He pursed his thin lips and looks questioningly at me.

"Show me," I said. I felt nervous about this. Why was Nelly looking at me that way?

Kagu swept his eyes around the amphitheater. Some of the monkeys stood. "Gentlepersons," —my translator was active once more, for he now spoke in monkey—"gentlepersons, I should like to display, for the human, the record of our mistaken intervention into the *Baleen Blanco* wreckage. And, of course, our dubious effort to repair the situation."

There came a gasp surpressed into a cough from the graybeard who shushed Nod. All the monkey eyes were on me. When I looked directly at one, then another, the eyes dip. I realized that Nelly's fingers held mine. Had something truly horrible happened two years ago?

"Show me," I heard myself say.

"Perhaps," continued Kagu, "some of you would like to review the matter with him. You must be interested in his opinion of this clumsy affair." I heard from behind me, near my ear, the soft, piccolo-toned cadence that got translated as "hospitality." As Kagu continued, the word melodiously whistled from monkey to monkey. "Then, too, this is appropriate to the ceremony of first contact." Those who stood, sat. No one left. I saw a flyer circling in the blue distance through the highest branches of the great tree.

Kagu tapped on a small keyboard, then looked up at me.

Show me.

XXXII _____

T HE PROSCENIUM became blackness
sprinkled with stars, as if an asteroid-
scale mincerlaser had cleaved a huge circular hole in our comfortable doughnut. As our
view wheeled, I saw Eros IV. And now I knew
as we swung back, now I knew as that blue-
white disk, an eighth the size of the Moon from
Earth, swept up, nestled amidst the familiar
constellations. Now I knew we were (they had
been) a few hundred miles inside Earth's perihelion. Earth. Though I bet Big-Blue-and-White

was going the other way. Our view carefully avoided sweeping further, but I knew the white fury of the sun was off that way. My hand went to my head as if to check whether my Melrick filters were at the ready, only to discover bare skin.

There was a gray dot in the center of the blackness. It grew. First buckshot, then pea-sized ball bearing, now separating into the familiar barbell shape of a small local-system boat. It held my eyes, I could kiss the familiar steel as it hoves up. Out of all this strangeness, this silly monkey greenery, this was solid, this was human. Oh no, but there's an ugly gash forward, must have holed the control/living compartment and taken out the inertial flight system. There's your class Z, billion-to-one-accident, that all spacers have to not worry about, like being struck by lightning on Earth. Federation registry number rho-nine-nine-seven-theta. I've been stabbed, the knife inserted at my crotch and ripped up through my guts to my chest.

Where's the big external tank for suit-refueling? This was obviously a miner's ship.

A suit arm rose as we shifted to helmet camera, wide jerky swings as we went inside the blackness of the gash. The hydroponics had vomited over the living compartment, freeze-dried algae spattered here and there, a large splat on the Gladden's "Computer Love" print. A close-up and I could tell that the algae

159

wasn't stone dry. The accident must have happened within the last couple of hours. And maybe, just maybe I thought, it wasn't an accident.

The old Klee abstraction, "Sinbad the Sailor," was clean. The Sleep-Me was shards, the decompression must have burst it. The camera pulled back out of the lift racks like there was something in there it didn't want to see. Hey, go back. Look there. Something there. I knew this place.

The eye withdrew, leaving the lonely charnel house. I knew somehow I had lived there. Look more, you bastards. The wreckage was pulled into some large bay. Hey, this must have been where they had found me. I had fainted the last time I ran into myself, and that was just some kind of wax museum construction.

They'd pulled a MAC3 suit from somewhere. The camera was just now focusing on it. But I couldn't see the faceplate from this direction. I didn't know whether I really wanted them to turn it this way. But now the view shifted again.

I wouldn't have to face up to that for the moment.

Deep space, once more. Sweeping up along the arc of Earth's perihelion. The twenty-foot-long external fuel tank loomed up, another MAC3 suit clamped to it like the lady riding the elephant. The sweep camera panned, shifted, panned again, collecting every view of the odd wreckage, dead still under this postmortem examination.

Centering on the MAC3. Scratched and bleached, this MAC3 had seen service. Maybe the one I saw in the tech section, or was it the first one, back in the little holed ship, that probably held me?

Anyhow, a good miner's rig. Something odd about the back of it. The gauntlets clamped into the line of tube fitting just ahead of the tank center of gravity, boots into the holder hooks. Hey, this wasn't an accident, this was something meant to go someplace, burned the tank clean, keeping balance. Must have been trying to get someplace, maybe Earth orbit, but it'd have been a year's wait before Big-Blue-and-White arrived.

The eye steadied in on the helmet. Closer. Couldn't see in from this angle. Moving closer and round to face in.

Not me.

Oh, I knew that frozen face, the camera catching each pore and line. At this magnification, nose the size your own looks when you're an inch from the mirror. Yet I knew the face immediately. Or thought I did. Who was she? Who was she to me? So familiar and tantalizing.

They're going to pay for this. Someone's going to pay for this.

The tank and suit were pulled into the bay like the ship wreckage. The suit unhooked from the tank and drawn off, laid on the deck. Dead as a whale. Now the camera centered in on the suit, zoomed in closer with a sudden sense of direction, like a ferret that had found a rabbit in its hole. The slightest of movement occurred in the suit's surface. An alarm rang. The camera shifted to the faceplate, already misted by condensation. Pan in with a dozen monkeys hurrying about, moving equipment in next to the suit, a flurry like you might expect in an operating room when the President's heart falters.

The camera zoomed in on the suit's tech dials. There, you see it, the dial was dead. Watch. Watch. Now one numerical beat. Watch. Watch. Several more monkeys came up. Some sort of listening device gently touched the faceplate. This was slow. The monitor dial beat again.

Oh, I knew what this was. Slow, deep hibernation. Though it must have just started, for her heart was still beating once every few minutes. If they hadn't picked her up, this lady would soon be down to breathing once a week. If she were picked up by Earth Sat a year from now, you'd have a serviceable body but the subtle neurological coding that made the mind would be blanked out. Would've saved the body, though, worth millions of credits.

162

If you update your mind tapes, it costs a couple hundred credits, mostly for the psychetian scrub. According to my Computer ABC's text, your mind amounts to a few million K bytes, about the same as the RAM of a midrange mainframer and you can fit the hard tape in your purse. A copy is less than twenty credits.

But you can't copy a living, breathing body, except by bringing up an identical twin like any human being, with a mind developing inside. What Botticelli painted is worth a million of Joyce's stream of consciousnesses. Humbling, that. Nelly was torn by that difference. Nelly. Her hand still held mine.

Way back in the middle of the twentieth century, Alan Turing thought that his invention of the electronic computer would make us respect the grace of the human body and its manual skills more. Poor bastard, the grim British court convicted him of homosexuality on his own, honest admission, and they forced him to take hormones that made him impotent. He ate an apple laced with potassium cyanide. Oh, stranger, that knows how accidental and fragile the connection between mind and body is, some of your software is in my circuits today!

They had the suit festooned with instruments. The pace had slowed and, by the dials, her heart was beating a little faster. They must be confident that they had saved her life, mind and body both. The faceplate condensation had cleared.

I knew her face like my own. Why couldn't I remember her name? What had I been doing with her?

Now some time had passed and the view panned to a group of monkeys, including Kagu, Nelly, and Nod. With the pan I suddenly noticed that several unfamiliar symbols had become a stable part of the picture, remaining on the lower right edge, no matter where the camera looked. As I stared at them, much larger English letters came up briefly, superimposed, like subtitles on Vegan documentaries.

This file of the actions of the Vineland anthropological team on April 30, 2111, is property of the Primitive Subjects Committee, Galactic Primatological Research Association. Any alteration of this record is strictly forbidden and punishable under GPRA Regulations 112.4 and 112.7.

The English subtitles disappeared. Nod maybe looked a shade younger and shorter, and perhaps Nelly as well. Kagu looked much as he did today except very worried. He spoke, throwing his paws up. I heard the piccolo tones of monkey from his lips, while the translator in front of my seat provided ISBM English.

"Well," said the Kagu image, "we have re

164

ally and truly put our foot in it. Improper first contact. We have violated the most basic rule of Primatology, no way round it." The camera swept from somber monkey face to somber monkey face. There's a splice. Eventually, we picked up Kagu again, still speaking.

"Remarkably, the female human is alive. We didn't detect it when we approached the wreckage because her suit'd initiated some sort of hibernation procedure, one apparently intended to save her body, though her mind would have gone long before she could expect to be picked up. But an explanation doesn't get us out from under."

"But Professor Kagu," said the Nod image, the ISBM translation echoing the adolescent quaver in his voice, "you yourself have pointed out that the humans have tried to send messages to the stars, thus indicating a willingness for first contact. Admittedly, these attempts have been occasional and unsystematic, but some were made a hundred years ago, before any of us were born. Surely . . ."

The Nelly image put up a paw, shushing Nod. She shook her head. "No, Nod, the professor's right. The ethics of first contact are clear, and Regulation 112 gives a reasonable specification if you're just interested in the letter of the law. We simply can't interfere with intelligent primitive life-forms—or metalloids, for that matter—unless they invite us to do so. To barge in without invitation is the worst form of cultural imperialism, just the sort of thing that led to Tau Ceti III, and may, if we're not careful, lead to it again."

"But," interrupted Nod, "they did try to send messages—"

"No," countered Nelly patiently but firmly, "we cannot excuse ourselves that way. That is how it all starts. A tiny minority, even one individual with her unrepresentative dissatisfactions, gestures at the stars with what may or may not really be intended as a message; and then we engulf the unrepresented whole with what they very likely don't want but won't be able to resist or cope with. Are we to land because some child, angry at its parents, screams for star monsters to come?"

"But you can't take the child's attempt seriously. The Sagan disk was—"

"Nod," reiterated Kagu's implacable professorial image, "that's no good. In the first place, the size of the disk and the speed with which it was sent suggest a no more realistic possibility of reception than the child's scream. Literally *any* nonterrestrial intelligence that was close enough to pick up the disk would have *already* known that Earth had a primitive technological culture. So the gesture was no more than the child's scream. But that's the least of it.' Kagu shook his high, delicate head and continued

166

"Suppose, just suppose, we take the disk seriously. It was designed by a couple of individuals, endorsed without much thought as a minor public relations gimmick. This is supposed to be an attempt at first contact—the most significant step for Earth since stepping out of the cave—and the decision is made without even the most elementary consideration by the leaders of Sagan's principality. And none of them even asked themselves whether they had any right to send such a message without consulting the other human nations of Earth!" Kagu's image flipped, heels over head, and went on.

"And the message on the disk is chauvinist on its face. There is a line drawing of a human male and female. The male is looking straight out, as if into our alien eyes, and his hand is raised, palm open in welcome. But the female has her eyes cast down and she stands behind the male, without any gesture of greeting. It is perfectly obvious that the message is 'Hello from us men and keep away from our women.'" Kagu threw up his hands.

"The very message," Kagu continued, "makes it clear that the message excludes half the human race. But it's not just the contempt for the other humans of Earth, whatever the whirgirs might say. There are, and have been, intelligences on Earth other than the humans. Nonhuman tailless apes. Lots of machine intelligence, even though the humans don't tend to recognize it, or allow humanoid-looking robots like the whirgirs. And even human 'anthropologists' have recognized that they have to consider the environmental effect of contact with an isolated tribe—whether their local fauna may be destroyed by new markets—so why should they not see that a decision to seek first contact must be a decision of all Earthian intelligence?"

"But," said Nod's tall anthropologist friend, "there are subsequent attempts. Another American attempt a few years later, and the several Russian messages of the 1990's, and then the secret broadcasts of the 2050's."

"No, all self-serving unrepresentative propaganda—a medley of songs with no provision for translation, contentious messages whose tacit content is 'Hello from the good Earthians who wouldn't mind some help in defeating our evil opponents.' It would be outrageous for us to take any of this as a reasonable initiation of first contact. Read my predecessor Momo's 'Considerations on Contact with an Interesting Primitive World,' in *Primitivity Review*. He wrote it as his inaugural lecture, when he took up my professorship some sixty years ago. But it's just as true today." Now the tone of Kagu's image softened. He stared off toward Big-Blue-and-White.

"Of course, of course, they are curious—perplexing, engaging, lovable—peoples. I'd love to be able to talk to them, as would Nelly, perhaps even more than I. Why do you think I've spent much of my life in this forsaken, lonely sector? I'm an anthropologist. But I am pledged to be a primatologist and you are, too, and we simply can't break the most basic ethical principles of our profession." His eyes returned to the assembled monkeys and his image smiled, dismissively and wearily.

"Besides, the GPRA will have our guts for garters if we further initiate first contact under these conditions."

The Kagu image turned, the camera panned around, following his gaze as Kagu pointed eloquently at the second MAC3 suit and that hauntingly familiar female, now suitless but draped in a sheet, still unconscious but obviously alive. Her right hand poked out. And her prosthetic tail. They were so damned familiar. "But," Kagu said, "I can't see how we can avoid their condemnation for this. We did pick this body up and it is alive and there's no way round that."

"Not quite," said Nelly's image, the camera turning on her, "I see a possible way around. We . . ."

But now the audio portion of the film stopped. More of the odd symbols appeared on the lower right hand corner of the image. Again, as I stared, what seemed to be an English translation flashed for a few moments.

Warning. As this case is *sub judice*, this audio portion is sealed, pending resolution of charges under GPRA 112.

Now Nelly had finished making her suggestion. Kagu's image seemed to be indicating agreement. The view circled as many monkey lips moved in sequence. There was a grudging nodding of heads.

Again, apparently, some time had passed unrecorded. Several monkeys carefully picked up the still-unconscious human female. What? They were, of all things, putting her back into the MAC3. The camera zoomed in on a whirgir, who was working on the suit's vital control circuits.

The whirgir, with Nelly and Kagu standing over him, was reinitiating the hibernation procedure.

Again there was a splice and I was seeing the suit, down-beating female inside, dumped into space. She's facing the same doom she faced before. As she zoomed away on her fatal journey, I heard a human voice scream. It was my own.

They must have picked me up from the ship wreckage. I must have been in that first suit, now stashed next to that replica of me in the tech section museum. I'm a spacer, asteroid miner by the look of it. But the woman—I worked with her, must have been her lover if my emotional reactions mean anything—they just dumped her. And guess who dumped her, whose idea it was. Nelly.

The monkey bitch was planning on me even then.

XXXIII

I SAW NELLY'S mask and, for a moment, didn't recognize it. I was still screaming. For a moment our eyes caught, her deep brown ones engulfing. What an animal I was to get sexual with her. With it.

"You killed her," my voice shouted. My hand swung across and she went spinning off over several rows of seats. Once more the savage brute and there was satisfaction in it this time.

Kagu stared at me. I grabbed up my black flying harness. I could feel the golden key in

172

my overall pocket. I hurled Kagu and Nod aside and ran down the central aisle and up the marble steps. I had to get away from all this.

"Human," called Kagu from behind me. "Ismael, stay to talk. I don't think you understand. And you don't know what's happened since. Sally's body—"

But as I heard that familiar female name, I flung a trio of frail graybeards aside and ducked through an exit and up marble steps, and Kagu's voice was lost behind me. The male name, Ismael, sounded unfamiliar. Never heard it before. Or was he saying "Is male"? But that doesn't make any sense. Forget it, monkey, forget it.

The point was mathematical.

Delicate-framed though they were, these monkeys were fast on the ground or through the trees. Avoiding a sharp projection, from where I'd ripped off the safety balloon assemblage, I pulled on the flight harness as fast as I could.

As I felt the lift in my wings and my feet left the stone, Nelly leapt out from the marble steps.

"I love you," she gasped, "whatever you think about yourself now. It's worth going on."

I understood her first three words—that's why the crazy bitch must have done it—but the rest made no sense, unless she thought I'd ever regret hitting her.

I swept into the air just above her. My muscles burned and I heaved myself upward with great sweeps of the harness. Within seconds I was a hundred feet above the rock garden, their small, frail figures spread out below. Dumb monkeys. I wished I had fangs.

I looked beyond the great tree toward where the falls had disappeared in the curve of the torus. The small flyer still circled there, now on the far side of the tree. Maybe I could make it to the tech section. The whirgirs were non-functional. I'd got an air lock key. Crazy to think I could make it, but the whole place was in chaos.

What choice had I got?

My driven sweeps, my compulsive breast-strokes, had brought me up several hundred feet. I started powerful, distance-gobbling strokes toward the great tree. For two or three minutes I was nothing but my arms made wings, clasp-ing air and sweeping it back in long body-length strokes. Up, spread, sweep back and pull. Up, spread, sweep and pull.

Whoa! I suddenly remembered the beginning of the scenes that Nod and his gang showed me. The holographically-recorded scene where some heavyset guy on a landing packet, com-ing into Narita, says, "Sally, even an ape knows what to say." Then, damn me, that female hand appeared, and now I knew whose it was, be-cause I've just seen it, before they put her back in the MAC3. So it's the same Sally. And that same heavyset guy went on to say that some meeting was going to happen in a week, on April something-or-other, 2113. So Sally was (is) alive two years after the monkeys cast her back into space. So Nelly didn't, they didn't, kill her.

Whap! My wings stuck together. I couldn't get my arms into the downstroke. The tips must be tangled together above my back, so I'm like a man with his arms tightly handcuffed straight back behind him. Except, except—and now my forward motion slowed and I started a gentle forward-falling arc—except that I was six or seven hundred feet up in the thin air. The sudden silence was deafening.

No safety balloon popped out to save me. I had ripped it off. I nearly pulled my arms out of my shoulders trying to get the wings loose, but it's no good. I was also trying to get the wing harness under me. The way to break a fall is to have layers upon layers of stiff but breakable things between you and what you hit; the successive breakage absorbs the impact. But it's no good, for the harness was lighter than my body, so it persisted in top position. I was helpless.

Several hundred feet up and now beginning to really fall, though still slowly. I remembered estimating earlier, that in this situation, I would, in a minute or two, be falling nearly as fast as a man on Earth dropping from a skyscraper.

175

This was femur-shoved-up-through-your-intestines time. Or skull pancake.

I'd flown about a mile toward the great tree, over the stretch of airy towers of the university, before my wings stuck. Now I'd swung round so I was falling headfirst. The vast rock garden was getting closer. At least I'd die instantaneously. A curious calm settled. Nothing I could do.

I now saw what I hadn't seen walking through the rock garden. It was, from this high view, a copy of Ryoangi, on a much vaster scale. I was picking up real speed, and it looked like I'd land headfirst into the one of the seven huge boulders that was closest to the formal gardens.

Off the way I came I could see a dozen monkeys in the distance. Several were running in this direction. Now, closer, I saw one that moved in a bravura version of the "swimming gait," using every advantage of foot, hand, and tail hold to move as fast as possible in my direction. Grace made into incredible speed. A spacer couldn't match it.

Some curve of my harness swung me around. I saw that the small flyer—Drink-The-Sky, maybe—was flying in this direction from the great tree. I'd hit long before she'd get here. The air went by me faster and faster.

As I swung around more, I saw the stone, less than two hundred feet away. I had seconds left. The last thing I saw was the speeding monkey, who had reached the gravel of the rock garden and still hurtled in my direction.

Whamp, whamp, whamp. Just before I hit the big boulder, something hit me a hard, but glancing blow, crumpling, absorbing, and I crashed into a series of ornamental pines. My flight harness ripped off, my arms pulled, everything roughed and bruised by a near endless series of impacts with pine branches and boughs. But I came up alive, twenty feet of smashed evergreen behind me.

But it was not just evergreen that's smashed. I knew that the first part of my impact had been taken by a frail body, a body that threw itself with acrobatic perfection, so that it absorbed part of my initial impact and deflected the rest away from rock into garden. Nelly.

I was up and running back, tripping over smashed pine but managing to keep going. There she was, forlorn, broken doll, limbs twisted impossibly, blood already spurting. Nelly.

My hands held her. I saw the bone of her upper arm was a foot through her shoulder, and thought, with mad irrelevance, that the white, red-tinged, bone was indistinguishable from human. Incredibly, the bloody, smashed mess still had a voice, and brown, engulfing eyes.

"Whatever," she said, "you think about your identity, you must go on. You must go on, my love, for that is the only way I can go on." She

177

coughed blood, shook her head at my attempt to speak. Now she went on in a softer tone.

"You have my voice, my words, within. Be hospitable to those, my best remains and as you ..." Now, though I still held her brown eyes, there is a growing cloudiness within them. She now spoke in her own tongue and I heard the translation, still more softly, from her wrist.

"And as you treasure these within you, so take your portion of me, my love, gladly at the last meal."

Her eyes empty and I heard a stir beside me. Drink-The-Sky must have just landed. I look up at her. Beyond her came up Kagu's face.

"Human," he says, and his eyes held mine while two monkeys scuttle in to check Nelly's invital nonsigns, "there's no translating. It is an important poem among us. 'Leave-Taking' is what the computer makes the title in English. It is the last of the great cycle, the concluding lines of a great love poem. I did not know it was a favorite of Nelly's, she had always called it sentimental. But she has been a mystery to us here, we never knew where she came from when she turned up as a student ten years ago. We came to feel she was a most important comrade though. She had the best credentials and came from galactic center, the old cultural sectors. That she loved you is sure, sir. And I am not sure you wholly deserved it."

I held dead flesh. Nelly gone, I held her bloody

container, her sleek-furred, elegant mantle. Nelly.

I took her translator from her wrist and put it on mine.

Snub-nosed, slit-eyed, Drink-The-Sky smiled down, warm, child-age. "My father, Think-Forever, make music with you, mud-man. I think be good for you."

Loved death in my hands, still warm, this disconnection of flesh, cooling. Her leg bones, which took the most horrendous inertial impact, were broken several ways, accordianlike. She was my crash helmet. Leave-taking.

Inevitably, the three solemn graybeards. They wanted her. Her body. It drained on me. I held it. Still her lean, now dull dead, head between my hands, so gracious. Did you see her streak across so much real estate to meet my impactive body? Did you see her go to meet her doom in seventy kilos falling mass? Did you see her set her body crumple to absorb impact and deflect it? Did you see her die for me?

Ever so gently the graybeards pulled my hands from her.

Leave-taking.

XXXIV

KAGU, NOD, and the other monkeys looked upward. They stepped back from me, eyes raised. Only Drink-The-Sky remained close.

Suddenly, shade and a gust of air, and the giant, brown-black flyer settled near noiselessly on the gravel. Think-Forever slowly folded his twenty-foot wingspan. His green eyes, larger even than the monkey's, were deep emerald pools, the irises catlike black slits. The monkeys moved still further back, Nod's face an expression of awe. I saw the same, or horror, on Nod's tall friend. Kagu looked toward me and bowed.

But the monkeys and the rocks and the sky faded as I sank into those huge green eyes. He moved closer. Though, given his structure, the movement was a difficult interaction of diminutive feet and huge wing-hands, there was nothing clumsy about it. The wings unfolded, their seal-brown darkness cloaking me. I had the uncomfortable feeling that I was, literally, falling into his eyes.

From a great distance I realized that he must be making sounds. His foxlike muzzle was open and I could see his tongue and mouth change position rapidly. I could hear nothing. It was like a silent hologram of someone talking. But, but I felt the presence of his voice on my skin, in my gut. His sounds were higher, or lower than my hearing, or both. His face and eyes continued to grow—like one of those endlessly rising cadences in music, which appears to go higher and higher in pitch. Staircases, Escher prints, Godelian proofs, stories within stories, multiplying paradoxes, upward.

His eyes, his ancient glittering eyes. There was lightness and cool laughter in them. The cool, light laughter of eternity.

Leave-taking. The words seemed somehow to come from his face. But there was no translator on his neck, where Drink-The-Sky wore hers.

And it's as if the sounds—were they sounds? —came from his muzzle, though there's no synchronization, for the lips had no harmony of movement with the English, as if it were dubbed.

You have my voice, my words, within. Be hospitable to those, my best remains, and as you treasure these, so take your portion of me, my love, at the last meal. But even as I seemed, in some inner ear, to hear these words, I also heard Nelly's piccolo tones in some still more inward ear. The strange feeling that I understood Monkeyese came again.

Now, somehow, I was swept through his eyes into starry space. I saw again, in awesomely vivid detail, that gashed mining ship. I swept, as before, into the dark control/living compartment, again stabbed—but it was like a dream, conjured from my memories—by the rho-nine-nine-seven-theta registry number. I saw the "Sinbad the Sailor" print: brightly colored, folded-paper-hatted fisherman, spearing abstract, primitive fishes, from his blue toy boat. But suddenly Sinbad altered, becoming Nelly, as I last saw her alone, bed-risen, before Kagu interrupted.

Nelly, my strange, wondrous, 'artificial' lover, who had been wrapped over the male/female, mind/body splits like a house of cards in a windstorm.

Her body changed to the blood held in my hands.

I was again in the doughnut sky, soaring with Drink-The-Sky. Flash.

Copperman was saying, "I wouldn't go in there if I were you."

I was back in rho-nine-nine-seven-theta. But there's no pea soup on the Computer Love print and the compartment was cozy and well lit. Back, two years ago, even before the accident. I looked through the coning port toward old Big-Blue-and-White. Home, even for spacers. A hand came up toward me. Sally's. I tried to turn my head. But you couldn't do that with memories. Flash. Scramble.

I turned, leaving the unwound copperman, and strode into the tech section museum. Past Egyptian, samurai, past eighteenth and twenty-first century. The MAC3 suit hoved up. And beyond it, again, my wax replica. Again it said, in this impossibly vivid, waking dream, "I am . . ."

Am I stranger to my face for only having seen it in mirrors?

Nelly's face, dying, mouthed those last words of "Leave-Taking." Somehow I understood the words in Monkeyese. Nelly, farewell. Nelly, I almost know who I am, and it won't matter.

Drifting. Drifting. Rolling slowly now, head over heels in the womblike darkness, silence and the distant hush, hush sound of air, in and out, in and out more slowly. (I could see my hand in front of the faceplate. I almost knew who . . .) Slowly. Must get . . . Slowly, dreami-down, down, down, done.

Again I was conscious of the echoing highs and lows of his bat voice, ringing and vibrating above and below my normal hearing, now done, and I, breathless and drained, like some avid music lover, in the orchestral pit, who had just heard the last smashing chord of Beethoven's Fifth. Alive.

His huge green eyes became smaller than the sky. The wings of night slipped apart, seal-brown once more, folding into his slim form. An expression, perhaps a smile, flitted across his fox face. He took three paces back. His wings swept outward, and with a gentle swish of air, he rose into the trackless air.

The "sun" was now low in the sky. Several of the monkeys were gone. Nod and his tall friend still stared, wide-eyed. Kagu, who had been speaking into some kind of communicator, broke off and our eyes hold. He's been through this.

"Ho, mud-man," said Drink-The-Sky, emerald eyes bright, pink tongue between tiny white teeth, "that be some music." She stretched out her wings.

"That be some music," I said. My mouth was dry and my voice, initially, hoarse. My body felt as if it had run a marathon. I saw dry blood on my hand. As the hand rose to my lips, I felt a calm beyond grief.

Farewell.

MY LEGS felt strange. As I stood, conscious of that controlled, easy maneuver, that lower-leg-management spacer's use, I saw Kagu, turning from his communicator. He'd some explaining to do.

But now I saw them swinging through the garden, a forepaw, a tail, catching here and there. The translator called them graybeards, but they're gray mugs to me, for the black facial hair that grays with age is too short to be a beard. As I opened my mouth to talk to

Kagu, I saw the last monkey carried the wooden box.

So soon?

Nelly, what'll I do?

From one entranceway or another in the university buildings, gracefully loped up threes and fours of younger monkeys. Nod and his tall anthropologist friend came last of these. Within minutes, scores of monkeys coalesced around the core of gray mugs. Oddly, I caught a glimpse of the antique copperman wheeling up.

The red, gold-embroidered, ancient-looking silken cloth flowed from the fingers of a particularly ancient and gnarled gray mug female. Slowly it settled on the red-stained gravel. Her outstretched arms now crossed over her chest. No one moved. Even the air was still. Dead still.

Like a priestess, the gnarled gray mug took the fragile, pale wood box, the host. There was grace and eternity in the transfer, as if this had been enacted countless times for countless years, each time as solemn and as gay as the first. She laid the box on the cloth.

The gnarled one, and the gray mug who bore the box, turned toward us. They walked with slow dignity.

" 'Hospitality'," said Kagu to them. His eyes shifted back to me. "Hospitality," he said again, in English. "How come you here, grandmothers?" said Kagu in monkey, his translator echoing in English.

186

But the gray mugs did not hold Kagu's eyes. They walked past him toward me. "We bear the gift," their translators echoed in unison. Their huge brown eyes regarded me without expression. Their next words were even more clearly for me. "As mother carries child, so child must carry mother." I heard Kagu and some others suck in air. The two gray mugs continued to look at me. Mute. Expectant.

"Hospitality," the word slipped unwilled from my lips and I heard the melodious piccolo sounds from my translator. Nelly's translator. The strange feeling struck me that the translator spoke and I echoed.

Now the two gray mugs spoke more loudly and their eyes circled the assembled monkeys, as if defiantly. "As mother carries child, so child must carry mother. And this is true however 'artificial' the family." I now realized that I'd heard that harsh monkey word muttered by several before this bald announcement.

The gray mugs turned back to me alone. They spoke softly. "You must join with us. This day we are double-blessed." Their eyes turned back toward the wooden box.

At their last line, there was a kind of gasp. Here and there I caught the flicker of a smile, a nod, the sense that the gray mugs had done something right.

Kagu said softly to them, "So, grandmothers

and fathers, we shall celebrate both unions together?"

The gnarled one looked carefully at Kagu and spoke again with a ritual intonation. "After the first contact, after the first death, we are ever one."

Nelly, what'll I do?

As the two slowly returned to the box, the other elders folded their long, fragile legs and took their places round the cloth. Several places stood empty.

Then one monkey and another gracefully folded herself gracefully into them. Soon only two places remained. The rest of the monkeys, Nod and the tall anthropology student, decorously sorted themselves into an outer circle. Only Kagu and I stood apart.

The gray mugs all looked at me. "You must join us," they murmured. It was neither request nor command, but a quiet assertion of inevitability.

Kagu stepped to my side. He turned from them His arm across my shoulder gently turned me, too. His slender fingers switched his translator off. "By tradition," he said in English, "the gift principally goes to the nearest relation." He spoke quickly and softly.

"They take you to be that because Nelly pulled you through your accident. Your recovery required a sensitive psychosurgeon, a harmonizer, and she, Nelly, played that role. Close enough to a mother/child relationship. An honor to you, sir, that they recognized it. Come, please." His fragile fingers tugged. I don't want to see the gray mugs' eyes.

"Is that," I said, "the reason they call her 'artificial'? Just because she helped a human being!" I spat the words out.

Kagu sighed and turned back to me.

"Shush," he whispered, "shush. We knew nothing about Nelly. No relatives. Nothing. Then we learned the only thing we will ever know about her past. She was an implant.

"An implant—a good anthropologist—qualified her as a harmonizer. There was no one else to call on. She had to expose her privacy to get the job." Kagu looked me directly in the eye.

"And she," he continued, "with her experience, had already argued that we shouldn't try to put you together." Kagu sucked his lips and shook his head. "But she felt that if we were determined, you should get the best help. Is implant existence really all that disturbing? She evidently thought so. Come." Again his hand gently tugged.

Nelly, I swear it by your flesh that I will make it for us. Whatever's coming, Nelly, I swear it. For us. Fare us well.

"You mean that I—" my lips said to him. And what was that about *first contact*? I heard coughing and shuffling among the gray mugs.

"Shush, human," said Kagu, "no time for

189

questions now. The graybeards have set the agenda. Come." I felt his arm, so fragile I could snap it, so gently insistent that I was powerless.

Nelly, so much, you did so much for me. A harmonizer wove together the mind and body of an implant or of someone with severe neurological damage. But the harmonizer did it through the direct experience of another's mind and body, taking the shakes when they don't mesh, spinning story and image that will join and repair, make discord into harmony. What was it that that big-time harmonizer, Candice Darling, said on the viddies after she'd given the wrinkled, liver-spotted, white-haired Lola Pons an eighteen-year-old body? *Harmonizing is having all the experience of being both a mother and a child, through birth to maturity, concentrated into a few days. I'd love to do it with a cat, if it was possible.* So said Harmonizer Darling. Harmonizer Nelly could no longer speak. Who, what, was I?

That gentle, relentless arm turned me. The gray mugs stared. Their eyes drew me to them.

A tunnel seemed to close round me. I saw nothing but the wooden box and an empty space round the silk. The tunnel moved by me and the space came nearer. Finally, I heard Kagu's voice in my ear. The earth came up to me. My legs felt like tree trunks when I tried to tuck them under me. Nelly, you can't ask this of me.

190

The gnarled gray mug stretched to open the wooden box. He filled a small, ancient, yellowed-ivory, handleless cup with water and set it in front of me. Other cups passed from slender fingers to slender fingers.

Inevitably, on the tiny rectangular stones, the tiny pieces of meat. No one ate or drank.

The gray mug who brought the box read the benediction. Our eyes took in the sky, where a dim yellow sun appeared.

"Remember!" said the gray mug's translator, "Remember! Though countless years have passed since we grew tails and became civilized beyond gravity, remember! Remember our primitive origins. Remember our ancestors."

Our hands raised our cups. I saw my fingers around the tiny cup without knowing how it came to be there. The cup went to my lips. It stopped an inch away.

No. I will not.

Now their eyes were on mine, their cups inches from their lips. They could not drink until I did.

"Water," said the gray mug.

The cool water was in my dry mouth.

An image of Earth—real Earth, old blue-and-white—suddenly appeared, circling the yellow sun. My heart pounded. Earth!

"Earth," said the gray mug. A bit of meat was already in my mouth. I gagged but the sliver had somehow dropped down my throat.

It is finished.

XXXVI

"REMEMBER," CONCLUDED the gray mug, "remember! After the first death, after the first contact, there is no other."

The tiny Earth continued to float in our illusory sky. I hoped it would not disappear as Tau Ceti III did. I'd even forgo the marvelous skyscape and sunset for that.

But the monkeys wait, their eyes focused more near than on the heavens. The gray mug now nodded to Kagu. I turned to see the end of a return nod by Kagu, his lean face inches from mine.

"After the first contact," repeated the gray mug. Her voice faded into silence. But the silence slowly transformed itself into low, almost inaudible, rumbles, and out of them came a wordless voice, a single note, indefinitely prolonged. Vibrations struck my head and torso. My skin seemed to translate these vibrations into sounds. My ears converted sounds at the edge of hearing into odd tingles and prickles in my skin. What I did hear is utterly alien and ancient, not the overwhelming, hypnotic spell of Think-Forever, but something similar, more muted, more severe, more ancient.

The wordless voice became two hologrammic figures, projected against a shadowy forest background, all laid out in the sky some hundred feet away from us, over the garden. The figures were blue-skinned, hairless apes. Both, though they stood upright, were heavy-built. Thickened by gravity.

One had yellow lines on his shoulders, the other, a red square on his forehead. They regarded each other nervously, at stone's throw distance. One held up a carved object. The other looked at it and nodded several times. Now the other held up a reed bowl and the first nodded. The two looked warily at each other, one stepped a pace forward, the other retreated; the other stepped closer, the first stepped back. The stone's

193

throw distance stretched between them like an invisible barrier.

The one now took the carved object and, openly and deliberately, put it down on the ground, off some twenty feet to his left. He returned to his original position, stamping and shuffling. The other looked on for a time and then walked toward the carved object. The first blue-face held his ground in parallel, followed the other, denied him the object.

Both returned to the original position, and now the other took the basket and put it off to his left.

Warily watching each other, the two circled in opposite directions. The first picked up the other's basket. The other, with a huff, grabbed up the carved object. Each inspected his new possession. Both sets of eyes came up and measured the other. Both nodded. With that nod, the throbbing music engulfed my body. The tiny hairs of my body stood up everywhere.

"It is," Kagu whispered, "the same every- where, though this is the simplest and oldest figure. Watch, now, the Generalization." I felt his slender, agile fingers along my shoulder, the fur of his arm warmed my back.

The blue-skinned, hairless apes, enlarged, moved, and faded, into two sets of figures, both harmoniously revealed in another masque of contact. One planet-bound, gravity dance emerged on a horizontal before us. In the other, a weight-

less ballet, figures entered from the eight cor-
ners of the visual space, sailed untouched
through the plane of the gravity world, top-to-
bottom, right-to-left, back-to-front. Imagine
yourself drawn into a tracklessly huge, three-
dimensional kaleidoscope world; one in which
endlessly transforming formal patterns, when
individually inspected, reveal and compact a
poignant myriad contact drama of the galaxy's
countless species.

In the gravity-bound drama, exchanges occurred between centaurs, otters, orangutans,
and mantises. Bright yellow centaurs with
touches of the giraffe and the caterpiller, straight-
backed otters with large green eyes and heads
larger than Kagu's, flame-red, long-haired orangutans footed it upside down, with arms longer
than their legs, fast-dancing mantises with
bright green exoskeletons, but obviously with
some high-energy, chordate circulatory system.
The exchanges worked through patterns of trust
and betrayal, harmony and discord. Through
it, increasingly, local discord was subsumed in
larger harmony, aggression finessed into friend-
ship.

The ballet disappeared into and emerged from
the horizontal display. The weightless entities
drifted, floated like sea creatures in a light-
liquid, or thick-air, environment. Purple octopi
with bright, wise, orange eyes, whirled here and
there on lithe tentacles; deep blue, cucumber-

195

shaped creatures, with stalk-eyes, blew themselves hither and yon; rainbow-hued patterns swirled, like elaborately choreographed schools of fish; pale-blue, dolphin-shaped acrobats cupped with hand-shaped forefins.

"After the first contact," murmured Kagu, "there is truly no other. Let us see how the graybeards celebrate you."

While he talked, the hologrammic display shifted ever more quickly from cast of species to cast of species, covering spectra of shape and color and texture, teetering from solemnity to laughter in breathtaking swings. For a split second, a thirty-foot tall Nelly smiled out from kaleidoscopic display.

Before I had time to react, an equally huge figure of the viddie talk-show harmonizer, Candice Darling, whirled across, her upside-down eyes, like twin moons, the last of her before she winked out like a soap bubble. Now I saw a flash of Kagu himself, and Nelly again, as they sent the female body in the MAC3 back into space. The spacer's body had a tail. Kagu turned to a whirgir and said, "She wanted her body to survive. Cut her an orbit home."

Suddenly this swirl of airy images was replaced by the packet boat cabin in the final seconds of the Narita glide path. The male human voice said, "Sally, even an ape knows what to say." That familiar female hand came up, and I knew it was the hand of the body Kagu and Nelly consigned to space. It survived.

The chimpanzee's hand moved quickly. "Talk to stars, Sally," translated the male voice, "and that's what the Syndics got to say, despite the Man-Firsters." I saw the heavyset, brainy, disheveled-looking man now. But now the view shifted round, past that familiar female hand, and I saw Sally's face.

I wasn't her lover, or her body's lover, back out in space.

That wrecked miner's ship was a one-person rig. Just the work suit and the spare. One in use sleep harness.

I had been Sally.

I had been her. Me. Sally.

The hologram played on. My eyes tracked but do not see. I listened to a voice inside of me. While the visual scene shifted from packet boat to municipal hall to an ancient Japanese gentleman pushing paper at what must be a Syndics meeting, I heard Nelly's voice. Only for me. A neurological recording, looped in before I became conscious. Outside me, they watched visuals of ship and message launching. A message would be sent that Kagu and his bunch could take seriously. A story of first contact unfolded. But to me only Nelly's voice matters, the private, silent voice.

"This is your harmonizer," said that voice.

Calm, soft English, with a high-pitched lisp, it tore at the center of me.

"When you hear me, you will have realized your new identity. Like me, you are an implant. And, like me, you have not only a new body but also a new sex. Your body came from Ismael Forth, who had a diving accident above our deep research station off Japan. Until we recovered it, we could do nothing with your software, the mind tapes of Sally Cadmus. So I suppose you are Ismael Cadmus.

"We respected your wish to send your body into deep hibernation, on an orbit that would eventually reach your planet. But Professor Kagu made the decision to retain a copy of your mind. Our decision to put you together is a risk. Always trouble harmonizing stranger mind and body. But I like to think that it's like first contact, an exchange of messages and bodies, cultures and habitats. Truly, we have worlds within us, their exploration as strange as space."

A diving accident?

Nelly's voice faltered. My eyes picked up the heavyset man and Candy Darling, who stood before a huge communications panel inside a large space station, possibly Finland Station, near the trans-Plutonian wormhole. "Let's do it," he said.

Nelly's voice returned.

"I am tired. As your harmonizer, I've put little bits and pieces of myself in you. Tomorrow you will become conscious. By the time you hear this, you will already have met me. Come and talk to me now that you know your identity. Until then, farewell."

But that wasn't the last of her voice. She spoke softly in her own tongue. She must not have realized that the neurological chip she sewed into me was still receiving. She was half-vocalizing that closing line of her great poem, as someone abstracted, who may unconsciously doodle with a pen. The translation leapt from memory, yet again I was struck by the feeling that I heard it in monkey. "And as you treasure my thoughts within you, so take your portion of me, my love, gladly at the last meal." In monkey, it sounded like a lullaby orchestrated by Beethoven.

Then a snap, and she was gone.

A diving accident?

Drifting. Drifting. Rolling slowly now, head over heels in the womblike darkness, silence and the distant hush, hush sound of air, in and out, in and out, in and out more slowly. Slowly. Must get . . . Slowly, dreami-down, down, down, done.

"Wake, human." Kagu's voice again, in my ear. He went on with a chuckle. "Is first contact as mundane as all that, my friend? Wake."

Drifting. My body—my present body—wasn't

in space, it was in deep water. That's why I went head over heels so slowly, so ponderously. Must have picked me up after my brain had lost enough oxygen to have been blanked. Or mostly blanked, because I still remembered that last scene, like the old folktale that the murdered person retained a retinal image of his killer.

"Wake, human," said Kagu. "Time for rebirth."

I opened my eyes. The show went on. Kagu himself was in it now, or rather some recorded version of him. His silver-furred hand greeted the heavyset human in front of the Finland Station communications panel.

"You have met with them?" I asked the more material Kagu.

"Naturally. First time we got anything we could call a respectable and representative Hello and Come Visit from Earth. Of course we responded. While you had your session with Think-Forever, we projected a simulation of me into your people's station. Not full first contact, because I was just an electronic projection. But several of them are on their way here now, for a little celebration, before the bureaucrats show up. Professor Mummett, the heavy guy. The chimpanzee hybrid, Go-Candy, of course she counts as chimp for her mind and as a computer-constituted implant, as well— quite a way to save the last chimpanzee, at least in spirit. Representative. That *and* one or two others."

I had seen a chimpanzee body in Nod's movies, with a heavy guy, and that familiar hand. Candy Darling was—had been?—a famous nympher and harmonizer. But what about Kagu's last smirked line?

"One or two others?" I said.

Kagu turned from my ear, pulled at me, and looked directly into my face. "Yes," he said after a moment, "she'll be coming too. Your counterpart."

XXXVII

HARDLY WERE Kagu's words out, when the sky exploded. A blast of white burned past. A dozen laser-sharp strobes pulsed ahead of a rolling blast of thunder. The sunset was detonating, a roiling blaze, the monkey who wanted to run the sunsets spread across half the sky, his eyes two huge brown-ringed, black moons, his smile a Milky Way.

The world went silent. My ears ached. My eyes burned. I looked away. Several gray mugs surrounded me—look like they have sucked alum. On some faces, blank startlement; the beginnings of fear. Copperman rotated his head, while winching it up and down. Just for the moment he looked more like an efficient track-and-fire attack robot than a cartoon from the Oz stories.

My ears began to buzz. The tall anthropology student talked excitedly to Nod. "Real sunsets is what he ..." Nod's voice faded. They looked about nervously. Everyone stared at them. Nod opened his mouth. But he didn't need to speak.

The fat, heaven-spread Buddha monkey raised both hands to us, an exultant orchestra conductor after a vigorous overture, before turning back to continue the concert. The slovenly loincloth and handmade sandals seemed almost obscene. Our disheveled Buddha's hand now moved to a prominent lever. When he pulled it, the smile that spread across his face became an afterimage in the full blackness of interstellar space.

"He's rigged access to the mirror, setting and rotational synchronization." The monkey voice, near my ear, addressed Kagu. The voice had worry in it.

As my eyes adjust, they took in the familiar constellations. No adjustment needed to take in old blue-and-white. Not the small illusion projected a short time back. No, this was the genuine article, low on the left horizon and motionless, while the stars high in the torus's sky slowly circled us except where they were blotted out by the opposite curve of the torus or obscured by the slender beam that supported the mirror.

Earth. Taking up a good stretch of the heavens, even bigger and brighter than she looks from the moon. My hands tingled. My heart pounded. Earth.

I know who I am.

I knew where we were.

Lagrangian libration point five. The most popular place in the solar system; an egg-shape, 200,000 miles across, where the combined gravities and motions of Earth and Moon created a "sink" in which stations or ships stay put, accompanying Earth and Moon on their solar orbit and stably balanced between them.

"You moved," I said to Kagu, "here for negotiations?"

"Here?" said Kagu. He held my arm. With the mirror winched to throw light away rather than toward us, earthshine was not enough to see well by yet. Looking the long way of the torus, from the inside, the right half of the sky was opaque. Must be where the real sun was, radiation ripe to burn our eyes or fry our skin, without heavy filtering.

"Moved *here*. To LG5."

"No, we've *been* here since the 1950's. Ideal

observation point. Where else would an anthropologist want to be?"

"But how did—?"

"A sort of stealth technology, spectrum-refractive envelope. Your instruments just don't pick us up or didn't until we cancelled our shield a couple of hours ago."

"You've been spying on our solar system for that long!"

"Oh, dear," chuckled Kagu, "such chauvinist words. Spying, eh? What do you call what your astronomers have been doing for thousands of years? Did you ever even think to ask our permission to look at us?" I could see his face clearly now. Something was changed about the constellations that pace by overhead. Though my body felt extra large and clumsy—for one additional reason obviously—it was aglow with a spacer's sense of orientation. I *knew* where I was.

"Well," I snapped back, "you certainly didn't ask *our* permission to look at *us*."

Kagu smiled quizzically and blinked. "Come now, my dear fellow, we simply couldn't have done that. Would have violated your primitivity. You have a right to your own private development, unless you invite us in properly."

"But you did come snooping anyhow!" Behind the faint and faded image of our sunset ape, our disheveled Buddha, still busy at his controls, the mirror was moving, blackness

205

against blackness, counter to our clockwise but slowing. Space, I know space. I was, will be, *I am*, a spacer.

"Human, snooping implies a possible intent to harm. We came in curiousity and compassion. We have a long record of successful first contacts and have rarely abused our trust. You have no such record, unless you count human treatment of apes and computer robots, and then the record tells against you. When you looked at our worlds, I don't think you deserved a judgment *on our part* of settled innocent intent. Your own literature often suggests a paranoid imperialism, a readiness to see contacts with other intelligent creatures as a prelude to warfare and conquest." The sober, passionate expression left Kagu's face and he winked.

"But that's," said Kagu as he held his hands palms down, "what it means to be primitive. The point of the dance you just saw is that compassion and cooperation, with a smidgen of reasonable caution, is the only rational policy for civilized creatures of whatever sort. Simple theorem of mathematical game theory. Your mathematicians discovered it a couple of centuries ago. But it takes time to sink in."

I suddenly realized that it was not just that my eyes were adjusting. It *was* getting brighter. I looked upward (from the inside of the doughnut, looking toward the hole and past the other side).

The gentle spin of the torus was definitively *slowing*. Started at a moderate half-a-revolution-per-minute or so—what's been making me weigh a comfortable dozen pounds. Now the rotation's down to a quarter of that. The mirror assembly, initially spinning much faster in the opposite direction, slowed correspondingly quickly. The mirror (or mirrors) faced away, a cluster of blackness at the end of the assemblage. Clearly, the angular momentum of torus and the mirror assembly, stuck at cross angles like a flag-bearing toothpick through the center of the doughnut's hole, absorbed each other's radial motion.

We had been spinning like a gigantic gyroscope. Now if I asked myself why the Big-Guy-in-the-Sky wanted to stop the spin, I don't like the answer.

My left hand lightly gripped one of the large, tall stones of the rock garden, one large enough, I now realized, that it must be anchored. My right hand casually cuffed Kagu's arm. My body recognized the approach of absolute weightlessness, and all its dangerous inconvenience. Three monkeys floated gently past me; one, whose casual stretch sent him skyward, grabbed for another, pulling her along, and she in turn pulled off a third, the three sailing up and earthward, caught by Newton's first law of motion until they hit our plastic sky—unless air friction extinguished their tortoise pace. My overall and flight harness rested motionless nearby. Okay for the moment, unless someone kicked them.

Evidently, my monkey friends have had little experience of deep space, for several already float hopelessly, the rest floundering, catching here and there on dust.

I replaced my hand with a foothold, and grabbed, as he floated by, the tail of the monkey who talked to Kagu about rotational synchronization. He was halfway between Nod and Kagu's age. A spacer, I hope, though he wasn't reacting quickly to full weightlessness. Anyhow, an engineer. His brown eyes focused on mine.

"How's he," I said, rolling my eyes up to where there still glowered the disheveled Buddha, dimly spread out over a good portion of the sky. "How's he going to try to do it?"

"Do what?" came the startled engineer's reply. Both he and Kagu stared at me.

"He's going to try to give us real sunlight. Why else do you think he'd eliminate our angular momentum?" I stared at them. Their eyes went up to our domed sky, where the gigantic, spectral-faint image of our would-be sunset maker smiled amid dials and buttons. In the name of Art, that fat monkey was going to fry us.

208

I've got that overall around here someplace, and the sky harness. Over there. Shielding. ASA Manual tells you that sixty straight seconds of Earth-orbit sun will blister skin, and just a few seconds now and then means melanoma. Eyes. I needed filters. Melrick gold-film filters.

"How," I asked again, "is he going to winch us around, so the sun—the real sun—will shine in directly? Has he got control access to the whole torus, or just the mirror assemblage, or . . . ? What can he activate, in there?" With my last two words I gestured to the controls that surrounded our disheveled Buddha, our idiot sky-shaker.

The light finally went on in the engineer's eyes. He looked back up and came back to me in seconds.

"No access to the main body of the station, no. But he's in the mirror assemblage control room, near air lock 4, D deck."

"Tech section," added Kagu. "A down deck from where we picked you up unconscious."

"In your anthropological museum?" I laughed.

"Take the slide pole," said the engineer, "at the entrance. One level out and you're there."

Above I saw the immense, ghostly fingers move. Buddha grinned as he pressed a final large red button and looked out on us in triumph and expectation.

"He's, he's," said the engineer, "he's winching

209

out the whole port mirror assemblage, override and maximum power. Or . . ."

Newton, third law. The action, extending half the mirror assemblage to port. The reaction, movement of the torus to starboard. Since the mass of the assembly was much smaller, the equal and opposite reaction of the torus could only be a few degrees—yeah, and just that would give us a fry of a sunset.

Annoyance flashed on Buddha's face. I realized that a panel of S-shaped levers had flipped out, a line of red lights blinking in parallel.

"Or rather," continued the engineer, "he tried to winch it out and got system override. You see—"

A maniacal grin on his mask, Buddha slammed the levers back and pushed what looked like toothpicks into the side of the contact points. A gasp of disgust escaped the engineer. "He can't, he can't—" The engineer's tone was that of the faithful viewing sacrilege. I shook him slightly.

"Can't he?" I asked.

The engineer looked upward again. Kagu and my eyes followed his. The last of the toothpicks went in and the once more expectant baby-giant Buddha again pressed the large red button. His whiteless-brown eyes, large as twin moons, were glassy and vacant. Had he been holding the red flag? "Can't he?"

"I'm not sure," came the agonized voice of the engineer. "The whirgirs, they—"

210

A blackness against blackness, seen in the disappearance of stars, was moving fast, up and out to port. The engineer and Kagu, craning their necks, saw it too. The slender beam that held out the mirror assemblage must be a good mile or more long, extending out to our left from the cross pieces that must anchor it in the center of the doughnut hole. How much give in the length of the beam? How much where it anchored, and where the cross pieces joined the body of the torus? How much motion once the momentum was conveyed to the torus? Oscillation?

Must be some real mass out the beam someplace. By any sensible design, must be a fifth that of the torus out there, for the mirror assemblage, rotating considerably faster, absorbed the motion of the main body of the station. Of course the whole unit was obviously built to have structural stability when in rotation. By the clumsy scramble and helpless float of the monkeys, I'd judge that it had been spinning steadily since 1952.

When I saw the shudder along the beam—an undulation in darkness—my mind heard a savage crunch. Several seconds went by before I realized that I hadn't actually heard anything. But something had to absorb the whiplash. Now the shudder was gone, but there was something odd about the beam. It was moving. It was no longer absolutely perpendicular to the torus.

211

The disheveled Buddha's ecstatic grin disappeared into agony. The controls around him rioted with red lights and button pops. The jury-rig tape work blackened and spouted electrical discharge. Though his body made a convulsive effort, the sunset maker could not draw his hands away. He slumped. The toothpicks lit up like birthday candles. His image flashed bright and then winked out, leaving nothing but Earth, stars, and the slender blackness of the beam and mirror assembly.

"I think," said the awed voice of the engineer, "that the beam is no longer structurally attached to the main body of the station. We may be safe from sunlight."

The inertia of the station had been enough. Rather than absorbing the mirror assembly's motion by turning toward the sun, the station had maintained its position long enough so that the motion simply broke the beam's connection with the torus. What the engineer did not add was that we have traded sunsets for a more serious danger.

Just call me Chicken Little. And remember that when the sky falls here, the air goes with it. Satellite mirrors are molecule-thin to conserve mass. Molecule-thin is molecule-sharp.

"There's a significant sunspot emission coming," said the engineer. "Naturally, I checked when I learned we were going to turn our stealth screen off."

Vineland had been stabilized by its gyroscopic motion *and* its "stealth envelope." Now both were gone and the motion of the beam had broken, or weakened, its connection with the torus. With large-surfaced structures, even solar wind could have its day. When Buddha jimmied the controls so that one wing of mirror extended, he created a solar wind anchor. If its present motion was not enough to do it, the mirror assemblage would eventually be blown into the plastiglass shield above (or out from) us. Vineland was a silly and perplexing place, this banzai bonsai. It was about to become an unhealthy place.

I identified the queasy feeling in my gut. Typical spacer reaction to large open places, particularly in weightlessness. I had no suit.

"Kagu," I said, "where are our human visitors?"

"Quite nearby, I'd think, though I don't know how we'll be able to greet them. They're arriving in a pilot boat. We gave them a bit of a boost from Transpluto."

Out of the corner of my eye I saw my flight harness drifting away, twenty feet in the air and climbing. Someone must have kicked it. I pushed off from the engineer and Kagu. The engineer's eyes flashed with fear but Kagu's followed me with a dreamy and attentive look—good-bye, my anthropologist, every man for himself (and herself) when the sky falls.

213

They cartwheeled off and my eyes left them as I flipped over. My hand grabbed the harness. Watch out for the sharp, jagged projection where I had pulled off the safety balloon assembly.

The image of Buddha in his control room throne had vanished. Though the awful face of the sun flared just over the torus horizon, the stars shown through the silicoglass as bright as they would outside. My neighborhood. And the absolute weightlessness that made you a direct part of that spacer neighborhood. Home. And I had been there all the time.

Nighttime. Spacetime.

A tangled round of helpless, fragile monkeys slowly, and noisily, ferris-wheeled on by, the lowest monkey in the group grabbing a paw or tail hold, only to be pulled away by the circular motion of the clutching mass.

The harness went on easily, sucking my hands into waldo wings.

I lifted myself into starry darkness, leaving behind small red emergency lights and huddling monkeys. Ahead, the awesome black limbs of Tree-elbow's masterpiece. Beyond the tech section. All ways, the comfortable stars.

XXXVIII

CALL ME Cadmus. Ismael Cadmus.
Howdyahdo and shake hands. My mind memories—Cadmus. And my body—Ismael. We introduce myself. Ismael Cadmus meet Ismael Cadmus.

I mean, what other name could I give to myself on such short notice?

Bit of a shock to change sexes. But, then, I had got used to this gorilla body before I knew what sex I was. And what's a sex change to someone who's already fallen in love with a monkey?

Cup and pull. Cup and pull. I heard the beat of my wings and the suck-huff of my breath. Otherwise, silence, as I coursed the night sky. Dim ahead the upper reaches of Tree-elbow's great tree.

Cup and pull. Cup and pull. Air scudding off behind me as I put my shoulders and back muscles full into it. Silence and crazy thoughts.

Ho, ho, let me go. We're human here, whatever the monkey-gods who made us. Honor our birth unnatural. Let the heavens stand up for bastards.

Let's do it right then.

Cup and pull. Cup and pull.

Right?

I baptize myself Ismael Cadmus, in the name of Nelly, Kagu, and Drink-The-Sky.

Past the spectral branches, gray-silvered by Earthshine, this black-winged angel fell. Faint in the distance I saw the tech section rampart. Some safety mechanism had shut off the waterfall. Otherwise no evidence of helpful activity.

What bloody damned fools!

Incredible idiots!

How could they let this happen? Like turning over a ship's control room to the tender mercies of a six-year-old who loves to press buttons and make things happen, preferably explosions, the bigger the better.

Luckily, there was some illumination in the tech section, so the rampart stood out against the dimness of the wall. I got a glance of an orderly, empty corridor stretching off.

I raised my wings into a stall, my legs swung forward. But I had overcorrected for weightlessness, so my feet hit hard and my arms were wrenched back when my wings caught on the rampart's edge. The wing material finally gave. I sailed forward into the corridor, past several doors, until I slowed myself by catching one thing or another, releasing the harness, which flopped off behind me as I finally came to a complete stop. I folded up what was left of the harness, the sharp edge inside, and strapped it to the front of my overall.

I heard alarms ringing in the distance. Otherwise, emptiness and silence.

Ship of fools, I'm in the leaving posture.

I EELED DOWN the two levels and pushed off down the wide corridor, slaloming along, slide-caroming off one wall and then its opposite, marking control as I dived through the passageway, taking the push-off of opportunity. (No handers or footers, though. Hadn't been off-spun for centuries. So door handles and ventilator insets had to serve.)

No copperman to gossip with, but the museum was still there, though dimly lit. Did a flip, caught a wall, and pushed myself off into an entrance. When the sky is falling, the quick get going.

I took the Cro-Magnon's head in my outstretched hands. Light touch now, let the mannequin absorb some of my motion without knocking it over. Swung around to the right. Let go.

My vector nearly sent me crashing into the Egyptian scribe, but I rolled and pushed off the wall image of the giant pharaoh, a glance of hieroglyphs caught in my eyes. The samurai loomed in the dimness, but my push off their prayer basin sent me straight into the eighteenth century. I knocked over a bewigged servant, sending plastic quail over the table into two well-ribboned gentlemen.

Oh, oh, too fast.

I blew my stop hold at the entrance to the twenty-first-century fresh room. I slipped, feetfirst; then my torso flipped over.

I sent the slimy-feelie goggled mannequin head over heels, and skidded across the MF plastilogo of the human superman triumphing over gorilla and computer.

I was around the sharp turn, floating gently, my eyes looking back into the mid-twenty-first-century. I drew my legs in, sensed the angular momentum, and let spin bring me far enough around. As my legs straightened, the MAC3 went by me. Still too much inertia. I hit myself (my double) headfirst in the belly.

219

Lucky they hadn't been realistic about mass or construction materials. The statue body softly absorbed my motion, keeling over head-to-knees as I righted myself.

"I am Ismael Forth, contemporary human male."

The voice came in English from the crumpled mannequin, who floated, nearly motionless, inches from the floor, a polite smile on his face. The piccolo-toned monkey translation came from a speaker on the ceiling. The translational duet went on.

"A large but not atypical human-ape male, my mass is three times that of an average person. In my primitive environment, my gravitational weight is fifty times what civilized men normally experience here in Vineland. Yet, in such a savage environment, I can jump over a barrier several feet high, or drop from a height of twenty feet without substantial injury. In a civilized environment such as Vineland, I could lift a platform supporting twenty men."

The face was not a perfect copy, after all. There was something in the smile that I didn't do. And the voice—the cadences weren't close. But then, they may have done a perfect copy of the body; but had not, naturally, captured the effect that my Sally Cadmus mind might have, joined with this body. (And who, pray tell, am I, that owns this mind and this body? Just wait and see!)

220

The voice went on.

"My people, a major focus of the research at Vineland, are heavily spread over the landmasses of Earth, and within the last hundred and fifty years, have further spread lightly over the rest of their home system and a few other systems." The animation of my bent mannequin ceased. A more impersonal speaker carried on.

"The Earth male," said the ceiling, "is a member of the dominant ape subspecies. His subspecies, whose development may be traced through the rest of the exhibit, has eliminated other ape subspecies, exterminating many even after acquisition of a primitive space-faring technological culture. It has also taken up a prejudiced attitude toward intelligent creatures of technological origin.

"Both attitudes are to be expected in a primitive people. We may expect these attitudes to wane. It is significant as well as essential that a chimpanzee and a computer played important roles in the Earthian decision to invite communication."

Silence now, but I had ceased listening already. My interest was the MAC3. It was no simulation. Or so I'd better hope. I pulled the damaged flight harness off the front of my overall.

The Zalder tool kit had the two parallel scratches. Got them when I scraped by two uncapped lugs on the *Baleen Blanco's* after winch. Flip-top's still quarter notch, the way I liked to keep it.

Okay.

Lithium hydroxide canisters full on green, breather and spares. Power pack, ninety percent charge. That's where the thrifty miner leaves it, unless she's topping off for a *long* EVM. Teaser valve said my old buddy can hold pressure. Dorsal suit check board all go. Beta-thermal zips moved like they'd been licked with graphite.

Hey, hey.

Okay!

XL

A RAPID, URGENT-SOUNDING buzz joined the less insistent alarms.

If you knocked a man-sized hole in it, a large station like this would take days to lose its atmosphere. But the sky mirror could slice open a mile of torus. Get them zippers open. Suit time.

Familiar, poignant, heart-wrenching, the body smell from inside the suit overwhelmed me. My throat is full. My knees come up in some

223

kind of fetal reaction, sending my head over into the suit's innards. Crazy time.

Crazy time. Out a moment.

Drifting. Drifting. Rolling now, head over heels in the womblike darkness, silence and the distant hush, hush sound of a buzzer, in and out, in and out, in and out, more slowly. Slowly. Must get ... Slowly, dreamidown, down, down,

No! Up then, wake!
Off, overall.
MAC3 in suit, prep, check.
Purge valve, check.
Lith-Hy function, check.
Idiot lights green, check.
Left arm articulation, check.
Right, check.
Zips down.
Left foot. Push. Bend the mesh. Tight, but it's giving. Okay. Right, now. Push. Sol, I sure had gained weight. And lost a tail.

Left arm. Right. Push.

Up helmet. Bend over and pull up, shoulders into it. The beta thermal flexed its stretch muscles, waldoing out and settling around a larger soft body. A good suit should take more than half the human-size range, and like any sensible belt person, I had bought a suit that could scale up a lot. Wonder what Birdy Edwards, back at Astra-Rig, will say if I show up to make a claim under my single-owner warranty.

Ease out. Shake. Still a touch tight. Must have hit the flex limits. Pressure up dorsal zips.

Okay, okay. All right now.

My breath was still coming in big gasps. I looked slowly around the museum. I must have hit my double sometime during my nutty period, for I saw his legs slowly disappearing into the twenty-first-century fresh room. My flight harness covered the species display sign. The golden-handled pressure lock key was caught in the jagged projection where I had pulled off the safety balloon. I refolded the harness, and clipped it, along with the key, to my suit front. Mementos.

Somewhere out there was a pilot boat. And people. People of a sort. Professor Mummett. My counterpart, Sally Forth. What Kagu had called "the chimpanzee hybrid, Go-Candy," the chimp mind implanted, with the graceful assistance of a computer, in a human body. Our Earthly Hello acceptable to Kagu and friends only because a chimp and a computer joined in making it. The Man-Firsters must really love that.

So I'm for the pressure lock. Any Earthian when your doughnut of monkey madness was about to pop.

XLI

THE PROBLEM was to find a pressure lock.

I dived into the corridor through what I now realized was the museum front entrance. Glanced back the way I came. Glanced forward, where the corridor disappeared into the doughnut curve some several hundred feet away, past myriad doors and branch corridors. There was a slide pole. Hadn't Kagu's engineer said that the next level out had an "air lock 4"?

I took the slide pole out, hand-by-hand, slid,

and flipped, my boots settling on the floor with no rebound.

Only I didn't see anything like a pressure lock nearby. As I slalomed down one way, my translator repeated the piccolo tones from passageway speakers. "Warning, all personnel. Automatic sensors indicate that station may soon be holed. Proceed to the nearest pressure shelter. Proceed to the nearest pressure shelter."

Did I really know what to look for? Oh, sure, I'd recognize an actual pressure lock. But what if it's located just behind an ordinary looking door? Ordinary looking except for a sign that I couldn't read.

I flipped and beat back the other way. Just past the slide pole, I got my first direct view of the funeral pyre of the sunset realist monkey. A doorway buckled, penumbra of ashy refuse. I was cycled to take ship air, while it was still available, so I smelt the burnt flesh. I switched to internal.

What a permissive world to let him get away with this level of destruction. What a . . .

Nelly had told me I should have just asked the tech section to open. I flipped my external speaker.

"Station," I asked, "where is air lock 4?"

"Retrace your steps past the slide pole. The fourth door on your left, with the green diamond on it, leads to air lock 4. Be careful when you open the door. I hope you can repair me."

227

Hope away. (And thanks, Nelly.)

Good advice, though. When I yanked at the recalcitrant door, it finally gave and flipped open, slicking dust over me and the corridor so I lost traction and cracked myself on the opposite wall, my flight harness and golden key twisting off the front of my suit. I got a glimpse of the pressure lock. I grabbed the key and watched the harness float into the corridor. No wings in real space. Hope Drink-The-Sky was all right.

Go, go.

Out the handholds. Key in. Easy turn. Lock opened. In we went. Easy close. Standard twist safety bar handle. Clockwise. Okay.

There was the external hatch, right opposite, out-ship. Where was the purge valve?

"Station, where's the purge valve?"

"Please check that your suit is fully functional. If you press the middle button in the array to your left, the lock chamber will depressurize."

Roger, wilco, and (soon) out.

"Note that several control cables still attach the mirror assembly beam to the intersection of the cross beams of the main body of the station. The whirgirs will reactivate within two hours. In the interim, it is vital to stabilize the beam so that the mirror does not impact the station's living space."

Tough.

The gauge that had been falling reached its stop point. I spun the external hatch handle. Open.

Stars.

"Farewell," I said out loud. But as I say it I realized that the Vineland computer couldn't hear me.

A cold tingle goes over me as I hear, faintly, the piccolo-toned translation from Nelly's translator, which still circles my wrist, inside the suit.

Hands to the hatch cowling. Up. Out. I took my leave.

S MY head went past the cowling, the endless, star-dusted Milky Way stretched my vision end to end, each stellar region drawing the eye as if it were the galaxy itself. As ever, the black was blacker than any imagination, the silence more absolute than any expectation. Dazzling Sirius rode high above the plane of the ecliptic, Procyon beyond her. Sunlight blocked by the beam that crossed from here to the opposite side of the torus. This nearby beam intersected the other cross beam at the center point of the doughnut's hole. Where the half-mile beam that sports the mirror assemblage connected with the rest of the station. Even at this distance I could see the rupture in the metal skin and bone that now marked that tenuous connection. And the beam was already visibly out of true, the laser sharp mirror assemblage already some distance closer to the body of the torus.

A second or two to take in this exhilarating view, and especially old blue-and-white, eyeing me, blinding brightly, along the ecliptic plane, far to my left. Eyeing me? Bigger, brighter, swimming up over my whole visual field. Eyeing.

Eyeing.

My crotch was an emptiness of tingling nausea. My hands had tightened white-hard on the cowling. Cold sweat on face and wrists. My wings were gone and I fell endlessly, evaporating into blackness. My teeth castaneted on each other.

My body was terrified.

Damn it, calm down. Down.

Though my mind was clear and my eyes drank in the familiar, homey space, my body overwhelmed their authority. I was going out. The tiny pilot boat peeked over the side of the torus. I saw a suited human in the boat rumble seat as the scene fades. I knew the face better than my own. As all began to fade into blackness, I heard a voice on my MAC3 wideband that I knew better than the one that came out of my mouth. I heard that and a strangely rhythmic girl's voice in reply as my consciousness went.

"Damn it, Candy, his last burst put us in a reasonable trajectory for line or magnetic warp in. You never free land on a station, never. Candy, what's the hurry anyway?"

"Be no Candy, Sally, no Candy Darling again. Gone, and not my fault. Just Go-Candy. And I need talk to my furry brothers, that's the hurry, ho!"

But now my fearful body took out the audio as well as the visuals. Now I was full and truly unconscious. Unconscious of the external world, that is. My inner world was noisy.

"This is your harmonizer, again," came up within my mind the familiar, comfortable voice; as if every fall ultimately landed in the eiderdown of motherhood.

Nelly.

"Though you are aware of your implant identity, you have experienced an intense form of the cognitive postimplant seizure. At least in milder forms, such seizures are common shortly after implant and self-identification. You must understand the seizure as a violent disagreement between your mind and body. Your mind, for example, might believe that you had just bit into a roast beef sandwich liberally spread

232

with mustard, while your body tells you that your tongue has run into battery acid. Your mind tells you everything is perfectly safe while your body breaks out into a cold, fearful sweat.

"That last example suggests what should comfort you. Your intense seizures are just an extreme form of something common to all thinking creatures. Take the case of an Oriental human, intellectually converted to Western ways, who has decided that something is *nourishing, creamy cheese*, only to have her mouth tell her *months-rotten bovine mammary secretions*. As such a person, you may in the long run desensitize the body. For the short run, better tell the body a story, like the vegetarian, forced to eat beef, who tells herself that she's eating fibrous mushrooms." The calm, high-pitched lisp paused and then went on, more personally.

"My friend, we implants stand over a somber truth. The primitive belief that mind and body are two separate substances is false. The mind is the program, the brain is what realizes and runs the program. The mind is the story the body tells to itself about itself. Just as different tellers may say the same sentence, or even tell the same tale, so different brains may have some, or all, of the same thoughts. So, you, my Human, and I may share thoughts, though our bodies are different.

"But with biological creatures like us, the line between hardware and software, between

233

bodily and mental aspects, isn't clear-cut. As your own poet asked rhetorically, 'How can we tell the dancer from the dance?' Worse, it's dancer and dances all the way down, for the body has its own hard-wired beliefs. My young, female implant body—my daughter, now myself—has its own wisdoms. As I revised her manuscript, I sometimes felt my pen move on its own, and better than my conscious mind knew. I hope you like my body when we meet." A nervous cough, and then that once more calm musical voice went on.

"More important, I hope you like your own body. Love it for me, my Human. This is the last of these messages, though it may be replayed if you experience a similar seizure."

Now her face came up full. Cheekbones so high and fragile. Lips thin and mobile. Eyes large enough to drown in. The voice was warm and dreamy.

"There is a dread, for the amnesiac, of finding out who he is. Perhaps he has done something so vile that his terrified mind has denied itself. Even if he has been a decent person, he may be forever exiled and forever tied to his former person. Imagine meeting an unfamiliar spouse, fumbling with the delicate texture of a settled life, knowing that you must, and cannot, be the man you were."

"But you, my Human, you can become what you decide to be, you are a blank tablet." Now weariness slacked her face. Her eyes went down and her arm moved and the words were a whispered aside. "Write something of me."

Now the eyes were up again and the voice cleared before the blackout. "Farewell."

I do not know whether the sweet piccolo-toned translation was her voice or the invention of my mind.

My eyes once more saw stars but the cowling comfortably surrounded my head. The pilot boat glided along fifty feet away. A heavyset, wall-eyed guy stared at me through his fishbowl and the cockpit plexiglass. Just behind him gleamed the bright blue eyes of a midteen girl, unaccountably a member of the visitors, though she, like Mummett, wore the transparent, passenger-issue MAC1.5 suit. Oh, oh, it was the implant harmonizer, Candy Darling. "Go-Candy"? "Chimpanzee hybrid"? Huh?

But my eyes looked for the occupant of the rumble seat.

HUMANS!
"Hey, you there. You in the MAC3. Glad to see you've returned to the living. If you can hear and understand human talk to us. What's happened?" I could see Mummett's lips moving. I nodded at him. My mouth was bone-dry. I coughed. I knew I was on circuit with him. Mummett's lips moved again.

"Hate to bother you, you understand, but you're the only thing we've seen moving since that mirror swung around. Nearly popped us. Like King Kong swinging at one of those gnatty little airplanes, eh, Sally? That, and *Lieutenant* Fitzwilliam's officious, apocalyptic bleating, like something out of Hollywood silver screen histrionics."

"Professor Mummett, sir. May I remind you that the physical safety of the civilian visiting party is my responsibility. And it's a substantial one, particularly considering that the aliens have the technology to have transported us here so quickly. My orders require me to accept your judgments—however imprudent I think they are—about the attitudes of these aliens. My orders also require that I protect you from clear-cut physical danger."

I heard it all in the voice. Regular Academy. Furthest thing you'd find from a miner. Not really spacers at all, you happen on them inside stations and liners, and parades. I saw Lieutenant Fitzwilliam now. His helmeted head came up from the after section, between Mummett and Go-Candy's fishbowls. Gray eyes, short-clipped blond hair, flush, well-muscled rapist and/or marine-type face. Stupid Linsberg Assault Suit. Not my idea of a savior. Fitzwilliam spat his sentences out quickly, School-yard Monitor to Baby Blue-Eyes.

"Professor Mummett, we have lost radio contact with the aliens. No attempt to take us in. Their station has sustained major damage. Any

237

entry is too dangerous. If the mirror assembly impacts the torus, decompression will send everything inside crashing. The whole station can be expected to explode. So, as I said, no entry. And if the mirror assembly gets five degrees more out of perpendicular, we will have to leave the area."

"Ho! Human, as last chimpanzee, I do what I damn please," said the girlish voice, high-pitched but with an unsettling rhythmic beat. "I only look human."

"Go-Candy," said Lieutenant Fitzwilliam, "I can deactivate your suit just as easily as I can Mummett's and Forth's. And I will if you do anything foolish."

Easy enough for Fitzwilliam to hike up to control three stock MAC1.5's; the Linsberg Assault Suit was designed to sergeant a squad of twenty soldiers. Bulky and clumsy, it also had all the dumb screws you'd expect in the latest flowering of military technology in a culture that hadn't seen war in over a hundred years. Probably the first time Fitzwilliam has had it on since Command School.

"Ho, Lieutenant Human," came the rhythmic adolescent voice again. I saw the blue-eyed, cherubic, midteen girl's lips move. "Best you not mess with Sally Forth. She got tail like these monkeys, right!? Monkeys, hah, human. Monkeys ride stars before you humans got metal weapons and clothes and kill chimpanzees,

238

hah!" Go-Candy, indeed. Politically, chimpanzee. A mind implant? Was "chimpanzee hybrid" the right term?

The tail flicked across my visual field, grabbing at the cowling. The rest of the suit and the face, lately my own, followed. Our eyes held.

Hold.

"I touched fifty feet down ship." The too familiar voice dropped to a whisper. Think of looking in a mirror. The reflected face moved and spoke but you knew your own face was motionless.

"So I eeled on over. Lord Kagu told us about you." There was uncertainty in her eyes.

"And he, about you," I whispered. Hold.

"So what's going on? And are you ill?" Her eyes searched.

"Yeah," said Mummett, "all mysteries dispelled, please. Bring on the supermonkeys. I love the smell of Nietzsche in the morning."

"Report," said Lieutenant Fitzwilliam, inevitably, "what you know about damage to the torus. What's gone wrong with the mirror assembly? Why no repair effort? Are they all dead in there?"

"Call me Ismael Cadmus," I said to her.

239

"**W**HATEVER YOU call yourself," snapped Lieutenant Fitzwilliam, "I want you outside and over to the boat straightaway. We may need to leave the area quickly." Beyond Sally Forth's wink, his gray eyes measured me. If it's peace and quiet you're offering, you're on, Linsberg, Command School, and all. A hot bath, a human bed, and a long sleep. Out of crazy world.

With a deft hoist of her tail, Sally eased herself aside, one arm gesturing me forward.

Again the starry expanse sang to me as my head moved forward through the cowling.

Again the tingling nausea, hands hardened to the cowling, cold sweat, vertigo. How stupid not to think it would happen again. At least I was still conscious.

Not really much worse than what many a normal nonspacer would feel looking down a wide-open airplane underhatch, one that bids fair to suck him downward, to be smashed by Earth's embrace.

Sally bent and her concerned eyes grabbed mine.

"Time's wasting," came the implacable Lieutenant's voice, "I think the mirror assembly has shifted a degree or two more."

What could I do?

What could I do, Nelly? Her words splashed out from memory. *Tell the body a story.*

Okay, Ismael. Okay. Okay. Being born was always a bit of dying. Go.

Drifting. Drifting. Rolling slowly now, head over heels in womblike darkness, silence and the distant hush, hush sound of air, in and out, in and out, in and out more slowly, heartbeat even, no sweat, the vast watery ocean so strangely still and clear, that one could see the whole of the torus-shaped underwater city. Damaged city.

Slowly, damn it, slowly. It's water, water

241

everywhere and not a drop to drink. Water, damn you, it's water.

Water.

Toe in on the cowling, easy smooth swing, and I was up (floating, damn it) next to Sally. Clean maneuver, and me without my tail. The worry was out of her eyes, though there was a quizzical look in them.

"Who's Nelly?" she said. I blinked at her. "You said 'Thank you, Nelly.' Who's she?"

My hand glided through the water to touch her suit. I faintly caught her last word through the suit-to-suit contact, the distant tinny sound that spacers sometimes make use of when there is radio malfunction.

"Just an anthropologist I know. Knew." Nelly.

"Lord Kagu," said Sally, "certainly makes a point of calling himself one. Quite charming about it. Claimed to be making a movie about the cockamamy way we happened to get around to sending a 'proper' message. Calls it *Tailless Savages*, or something like that. Hope he's all right. What has been going on in there?"

Well, what did the savage say to his fellows after two days in the lair of the anthropologists?

"The robots—whirgirs—who do the engineering and maintenance are shut off. On strike or whatever. May start up again in a couple of hours. But ..." I gestured toward the mirror assemblage. It *had* moved further starboard out of true. Port extension, blindingly bright,

242

caught the full pressure of the sunlight. I gave it fifteen minutes before the starboard surfaces come down on the living space of the torus like a razor on a soap bubble.

"Sally," said Lieutenant Fitzwilliam, "return to boat. Bring this Ismael Cadmus with you. Quick! We've got to get out of here."

"Ho! Lieutenant Human," said Go-Candy, her arm to Fitzwilliam's back, "you not leave monkeys so quick. Help them." Her bright blue eyes implored the relentless Fitzwilliam. He shook her arm aside. Slender and fragile against the metallic bulk of his Linsberg, her arms went to his chest. One inexorable movement of his armored arm flung her into her seat, breath whooshing.

"I help my furry brothers," gasped Go-Candy. "You not control me."

"Look, freak," said Fitzwilliam, "I've heard your whole revolting story. Candy Darling's mind going into neurological collapse and you got a genetic disease, so Candy gets the docs to implant your scum-ware into a human body. You're a brain-dead human with monkey twitches. Cargo."

"You not control me," said Go-Candy, with an adroit wriggle that temporarily refuted Fitzwilliam. Shooting out from under him, she pushed off a startled Mummett and hit the business end of the control panel.

"We're coming," said Go-Candy, to everyone

243

or no one. She (he?) gave a glance our way and briefly fired the aft and dorsal control rockets. Suddenly, her body went rigid. I saw that Fitzwilliam had worked the controls on the front of his Linsberg. He plucked up Go-Candy.

"Release my suit, shit for head," screamed Go-Candy, "you—" And then her voice went, as Fitzwilliam pushed another button. He glared at Mummett and shoved Go-Candy's paralyzed form back into the pilot boat's cargo compartment. So much for mutiny.

In a couple of seconds, I could see that Go-Candy's aim had been good. Looked like the pilot boat, gliding forward at a leisurely pace— two or three feet a second—would soon graze the stanchion where Sally and I stood.

"Brace your back, against the station, here," I said to Sally demonstrating my own advice, "legs up, so we can take her."

Fitzwilliam's face looked nervous under the heavy faceplate. He had realized that the boat was going to hit the torus. He had locked the controls from his Linsberg before grabbing Go-Candy. Now he released them and looked anxiously at us, ready to fire.

"Don't," I said.

Just as with water-going boats of old, you always use lines or mechanical arms for docking. But the role is even more important in space, for deep space structures are incredibly fragile, given the masses involved. A water-going boat has to stand up to wave and wind. No perceptible waves in space and the only wind is light itself. And you build everything with the minimum of material.

"We'll walk her through," I said, putting all the confidence and authority I could into my voice. I hoped Fitzwilliam realized that the only control rockets that would deflect the pilot boat would fire in our faces. Besides we could do a neater job.

"Reach out to it," I said to Sally, "and start walking backward in place the moment it touches. Don't let your feet get caught." The pilot boat massed less than its passengers.

The belly of the boat loomed up. The angular momentum toward the torus had to be only a small percentage of the velocity. Feet do your stuff.

Midpassage I felt the deck beneath my back buckle a little. But a few more paces, and we'd legged it through. The pilot boat glided on past us, Fitzwilliam and Mummett lost to view. But Fitzwilliam was hardly inaudible.

"Sally," he ordered, "I want you on board quick. And bring Mr. Cadmus, as I said. I don't want to burn you when I fire the main rocket. We're getting out of here." Fitzwilliam craned himself up so we could see him looking back from the boat.

"But what," I said, "about ..." My hand swept in a semicircle. If the chimp cared, why not I, who had even had a tail. Fitzwilliam's gray eyes drilled into me. There are beads of sweat on his forehead.

"And you, mister," he spoke through my question, "the one thing I know for sure about you is that you've been under alien control. So . . ."

When I heard that "so," I caught Sally's eyes, throwing everything into my expression that I dared not say aloud. *Watch me*, my eyes said. I moved so that her body shielded me from Fitzwilliam. I brought my hand up to my ventral panel and deliberately flipped the radio output switch off. *You too*, my lips and nod said just as paralysis hits me.

". . . you will understand why I am deactivating your suit," continued Lieutenant Fitzwilliam. "And no tricks from the rest of you. This is a command decision. Tote him back here, Sally."

Water, damn it, it's water.

For I was truly helpless now, my waldos rigid. I could wiggle my toes, twitch my nose, and waggle my tongue.

Keeping her back to Fitzwilliam, Sally locked eyes with me and carefully flipped her own radio off. Then she reached over, ostensibly to "tote" me, but with a lot more suit-to-suit contact than necessary. Bright lady. Deserved my body.

"He's been acting paranoid all along." Her

246

voice tinny but clear. "What have you got in mind?"

"Don't use your tail when taking me in. Don't do anything to make him think about it."

For the real spacer, the yearlong bioprosthetic operation was worth it. Beyond gravity, a prehensile tail is invaluable. Already I felt as envious—and with more reason—of Sally's tail as I had been of the monkeys'. But Lieutenant Fitzwilliam wasn't a real spacer, so it wouldn't be an automatic part of his thinking. Or so I hoped.

"Sally," I said, "are you good enough with your tail to reach behind him and tap in the top two buttons on his dorsal check board?"

"I sure can try. The tail often seems to know how to do things."

Yeah, I could believe that.

So she took me in her arms, took the measured push off, and I sailed, paralyzed, through the oceany womb, after the pilot boat, which had already glided on a score of feet.

Tell the body a story.

Did you see Nelly streak across so much real estate to meet my impactful body? Did you see her go to meet her doom in seventy Earth-kilos falling mass? Did you see her body crumple to absorb impact and deflect it?

How often did you think of one lover while in the arms of another?

Water, I tell you. Watch the damaged underwater city flow by.

Watch the sword of heaven descend.

Only ten degrees out of true but it will start
to pick up speed real soon. A dozen minutes.

LIKE A camera, I only see what I'm pointed at. Some, mostly verbal, confrontation was going on between Fitzwilliam and Mummett about the Lieutenant's treatment of Go-Candy. A large Linsberg arm landed on Mummett's stomach and his voice whooshed into silence.

Sally flipped round to land feetfirst on the pilot boat, and now my head faced away. Anyhow, things were tense.

"Sally," said Fitzwilliam, "I want you to stow

Mr. Cadmus in the after compartment, along with Go-Candy. The zombie got too hyper. I've deactivated her suit and her voice circuits. No private heroics, please. We can sort out all this when we get back to civilization."

"Okay," said Sally, must have turned her speaker back on. The torus swept by me. Tail, do your stuff.

"Let me give you a hand," said good old Lieutenant Fitzwilliam. It was the last we were to hear from him.

"Got 'em," said Sally.

"Hoot," hooted Go-Candy.

Gloriously, I felt control flood back.

"Hoot, HOOT, *HOOT!*"

I whipped round, one hand on the open hatch of the boat. Fitzwilliam's huge Linsberg Assault Suit did a dance inches from me. I could see Fitzwilliam's furious face mouthing the word "mutiny." While I had switched off his output radio, he had the wideband to hear us, whether or not he wanted company.

Sally and I eased the Linsberg away from the boat, avoiding the spasmodic limbs. It drifted away ever so slowly, jerking through a mad routine, like a marionette whose manipulator was palsied. Except that the manipulator was the locked-in suit articulation check routine. Until and unless we got around to doing something (which may just be a while), poor Lieutenant Fitzwilliam would float toward eter-

250

nity, his waldos endlessly knee-bending and saluting, relentlessly working through the articulatory test circuit again and again and again.

I could have gone on about dozens of other ways of messing up a Linsberg, but I'd got a sky to stop falling.

"Jerking military jackass," murmured Mummett, *"ad astra per aspera."*

Unfortunately, we were going to have to pull Lieutenant Fitzwilliam back from his difficult journey if we wanted to get the pilot boat operating. A moment with boat's controls showed me they were now locked to his damn Linsberg. Sally's eyes took it in.

"Brother," she said, with a tense laugh, "I sure hope your muscles are as good as when I had 'em."

"You'd help?"

"Me too, human," said Go-Candy. In repose, her blue-eyed, fair-skinned face was your perfect Alice in Wonderland. But the voice and the play of expression bring out something wilder and more wily. Sally and I looked at our chimp-minded, human-bodied volunteer.

"Who," said Go-Candy, her blue eyes sparkling, "but these monkeys tell me where be other chimpanzees? Or how clone up my old cells with no gene screwup?"

Professor Mummett giggled. "Hate to have him as my only excuse," he said, gesturing to Fitzwilliam's retreating figure, "but anything to thwart pighead. I'll go with you unnatural idiots." Mummett managed to get to the hatch, saluted, and almost lost his grip, flipping upside down relative to us. "Clumsy as I am," he said, "you'll have to carry me there, but I do have some muscle."

"Now," I said, grabbing Mummett and taking a good push off. Mummett in my lap and the breakage square in my helmet cross hairs, I fired two seconds of pseudohylox out the suit's dorsal jet. Sally, lugging Go-Candy, used more fuel and rapidly closed. She'd need to absorb some momentum when she hit the torus crosspiece. But, then, Go-Candy was hardly the mass of Mummett.

"Speaking of unnatural idiots," I said, "how come they sent you guys as the first face-to-face contact? Kagu told me that you were crucial in getting the first contact invitation sent, or sent properly. But you don't seem to be typical ambassadorial material, no offense intended."

"None taken, son," said Mummett, his massive head swiveling in his fishbowl to grin at me. " 'Course the biggies are all squealing up to the trough on this, everyone from the Chancellor of Oxford to old Fujiwara, of the Ecological Syndics, all trying to get seats for the biggest and most exclusive occasion of the century. The *real* embassage is coming in a couple of hours, *if it's safe.*"

An upheaval that I eventually recognized as a wink convulsed Mummett's flush, lopsided face. Mummett, the one "natural" mind/body pairing among us, may be the worst mismatch. Maybe, for "natural" nonimplant persons, it can be like what happens to two sisters, or two brothers, grating against each other to produce more differences than if they were raised apart. And this demi-Quasimodo, quantum-mathematicizer, who can say he's not a stranger symmetry than Go-Candy? Aren't we all implants? Software on temporary assignment.

"We're just," went on mismatched Mummett, "some casual unofficial, non-first-contacting unvisitors, don't you know. Expendables pushed forward to do the dangerous work, while the official heroes go safe second and claim first— like the first cosmonaut, who was a dog, and the first astronaut, who was a chimpanzee." Naturally, Mummett's last phrase was declaimed in unison, and much more loudly, by Go-Candy's strangely rhythmed soprano.

"Just maybe," came Sally's cool contralto, "we're here first because Kagu insisted. Hard to turn down an invitation from the galactic culture. The agreement is that we're to be off-stage when the official first-contact embassage appears. Can't have first contact when there are prefirst contacters around, any more than you could've had the chimpanzee Enos arm-in-arm with John Glen in the parade celebrating

253

the 'first' astronaut to circle the earth. Anyhow, here we are."

"They were expendable," Mummett declaimed in mock-heroic tones, echoing all the bunker-enclosed generals of history. He turned his head back to the rapidly approaching crosspiece.

"As old Archimedes said," said Mummett, his voice now as carefree as someone punting down Oxford's ancient river, "give me a lever long enough . . ."

WE DID have a place to stand but the only levers we had were bodies. Human bodies.

Sally sailed in just ahead of me, settling hard but firm into the crosspiece, a few feet from the ripped shell and the smash of structural struts. Go-Candy grabbed a handhold and looked back at me. Confident movement. No trouble with her.

And we had a good fulcrum for the mirror assemblage mast. The intact power lines that still held the mast to the crosspieces of the torus were more like girders, flexing freely only where mast and crosspieces joined. The heavens were well connected. The crosspieces lipped in a few feet before they reached the mast. Just the place for a few strong backs.

I did a last second flip, feetfirst into the starboard arc of the lip, already squinched by the relentless motion of the mirror assembly mast. Mummett's bulk was in my arms above my head, slung back so I took his inertia down the line of my spine as my feet and legs settled in. Piece of cake.

Now the hour of the brute. So, my graybeards and juveniles, Kagu and Nod, a primitive ape such as I could "lift a platform with twenty men." Finally my muscle-bound gravity-bred clumsiness had its place, and strangely, in full weightlessness.

I settled my back into the lip, eased my feet into a metal rib on the mast, and began to push. Sally and Go-Candy settled in next to me. Mummett, who I'd put into position with the last of his inertia, finally saw the task. After a slip that nearly sent him cartwheeling after Fitzwilliam, Mummett got himself firmly braced.

"Push."

This was nothing like legging the pilot boat. The mechanical disadvantage was enormous.

Image someone trying to stop a Douglas Fir from falling over by bracing it with his body. And the mast was several times greater, longer, and massed at least as much, if not a lot more.

Of course what we're fighting was the swiftest and most intangible of winds—light. That and the accumulated inertia of a mast already in motion. Still, the human body, pound for pound, versatility for versatility, was the best servomechanism around. Built tough, not like the airy fragility bred beyond gravity.

Push.

Push.

"Ismael," came the voice once my own, "let your back full into the curve beneath you. Don't let yourself arch it. Easy on the left knee."

And she was right. Knew my body so much better than I—but isn't that what spouses and novelists have always, and rightly, imagined? Isn't your body more unfamiliar to you than your lover's?

Push.

For a second, the mast moved back, but then I realized it is some give in my foothold.

I want my old body back.

"Damned puny human muscles," said Go-Candy.

Second best servomechanism. She's a plucky little bastard. Wonder if the chimpanzee mind was asking more of that adolescent human musculature than any human mind could. Candy

257

Darling had said that she'd like to have the body of a cat. She'd ended up donating her body to a chimpanzee mind. Beauty saved the beast indeed.

And Sally mourned her harmonizer, Candy Darling, and I mourned mine. I twisted my head and found Sally's eyes. "Does the tail," I said, "still go tingly when the tip hits a magnetic field?" She smiled a nod and I was sure the tingle still had the sexual quality it had had for me. Eyes.

"Despite the poets," puffed Mummett, "you hold up the sky with your feet, not your shoulders."

Push.

I didn't like this. Almost imperceptibly but inexorably, the mast still moved starboard, cleaverlike mirror on its end.

"Wedge up," I said, "and straighten. Don't try to push it. Make your skeleton the brace."

Slowly. Slowly. I could feel the mass settling in, slowly and inexorably. Hold it. Hold.

Feel the spinal cartilage squeezed Knees locked, beginning to take real punishment.

"Are they good people?" came Sally's voice from a distance. Steady, soft, reflective.

How should I answer?

That our gods had always been a metaphor for extraterrestrial intelligence? That heaven was always beyond gravity? That any human child wanted to fly?

That a monkey-god is my only father? That my exquisite three-day mother/lover lived and died to bear me?

Hold.

We'd bought them a few minutes, nothing more.

When would we give?

Hold.

"I MUST SAY," came the mechanically paced ISBM English, "I warned you about going into that museum. But I am glad that someone's been minding the store." I heard a multitude of ticktocks and metallic hiccups.

Craning my head back, I saw copperman's absurd head.

"My biological ones," he said, "just hold a bit longer. I play a character from your own stories." He raised his sticklike arms. Suddenly, his large, spherical torso exuded several steel rods that converted his flimsy arms into the business appendages of a forklift. Even more formidable rods projected downward and anchored into a structural rib a few feet beyond the lip where our backs rested. Behind the amusing cacaphony of ticktocks, I heard the faint, solid whir of real machinery.

"Okay," he said, "I can hold it until the whirgirs arrive."

Dazed, I stretched my bruised frame.

"Well, introduce me," said copperman.

"What," I said, "happened to 'equalization is civility.' You told me you were weak as a monkey."

"Well," copperman grinned mechanically, "us Bootes folks usually don't hold with piffle. Never trust an artist, that's what I always tell the monkeys, and apes like you." Copperman's eyes widened. "You don't think," he winked, "that Kagu and the rest will be terribly angry about it, do you? Least not any more than they'll be irate at you for savaging a museum exhibit and running off with a primitive artifact. Okay?"

"Okay," said Sally.

"THIS ALLOWS you to fly?" said Sally, picking up the flight harness that I'd left just inside the pressure lock.
Leaving the mirror assemblage in copperman's capable appendages, we'd sailed back to pressure lock 4. The artist cum forklift, soon to be relieved by a repair party of reanimated whirgirs, smiled and eye-popped over his spherical back, as we silently coursed the star-splashed blackness.

Easing my way out of my gray-skinned MAC3,

262

I twisted some combination of the back muscles and my left leg. After rechecking pressures and opening the inner lock, I'd been hurrying too fast to catch up with the others. A red-hot pain shot from ankle to midback. My gasp filled the floating confusion of partially empty suits and partially freed bodies. Unsuited Sally stared at me upside down, her face rigid, and beads of sweat on her forehead.

Though the passenger MAC1.5's were (more or less) transparent, I felt suddenly overwhelmed by her physical appearance. My muscular spasm disappeared as her face swung around. Her eyes covered me. This was the first time she'd seen anything but my face, through the MAC3 fishbowl.

Everything disappeared around us.

With a convulsive effort, Sally tore her eyes from mine. I followed her gaze to the flight harness, which floated spectrally just inside the hatch leading into the station. I told her what it was for.

And so, after her skeptical comment, her fingers inspected the harness. An instant too late I saw her fingers touch the rib where I'd ripped off the safety balloon. I saw the jagged projection move across her right trigger and middle fingers.

And I *felt* it penetrate. Pain.

Sharp, nasty, though hardly deadly, pain.

And I didn't feel the pain in my (current)

fingers. I felt it in Sally's fingers. Right where the damage occurred. Felt it as real as pain you've ever felt. Felt *it* and felt it over *there*, right in her fingers.

She pushed the harness away and brought her gashed fingers in front of her face. Her eyes caught the strain on my face and widened. Then a smile flitted across her lean, high-boned face.

"We aren't hurt bad," she said.

Am I stranger to this face for only having seen it in mirrors?

For those gray-green wolf eyes sparkled and engulfed unfamiliarly like long-hidden jewels, glimpsed only in candlelight, brought now into bright day. I see my eyes in hers, and her's in mine, and each in each again, as two mirrors multiply and miniaturize into infinity.

Through the blue overall, the long muscle of her back feels the fingers of my right hand. Cold fingers stroke the hair that rises up prickly on the back of my neck. Lips call lips on lips. I feel our breasts against our chest. The smell that was stale in the MAC3 is fresh. Going home. Home.

I do not know where one body ends and another begins.

On the basis of coyly unspecified evidence, the male Victorian MD confidently asserted that sexual orgasm culminated in a brief period of unconsciousness. He should have tried kissing himself.

A delicious giggle sailed up between us, like champagne dacca in the spun-diamond glasses of New Holland. A cultivated cough brought us back eye-to-eye.

"Is male," said Sally and lowered her eyes mock-demurely.

"Asteroid Sally," I replied, remembering the joking of the guys at Astra-Rig. The spin had begun to come on while we embraced and just a pound or two from the invisible hand had eased our feet to the floor.

"Again your servant," came that familiar antique voice, "and again you do seem to be enjoying yourself and again I need your help. Though this time it's your own august human plenipotentiaries and not the whirgirs, who are doing their best to tidy up."

I had forgotten how tall and grave Kagu was. Now that he had our attention, he bowed to Sally.

"Madam, I have met you in the flesh before. I now welcome you in spirit."

XLIX ─────────────────────

"**I** COME IN peace for all mankind. Take me to your leader," said Chancellor Harold Gambier Household. It was his second sentence that really started the fire, until Sally found the way to put it out. But perhaps I should start with the Mummett-Fujiwara-and-the-rest-of-us planning session right there at air lock 4 that preceded the would-be *official* first contact meeting.

"As I said," said Mummett, "the biggies are all squealing up to the trough on this one.

Really your fault, Kagu, so I'm afraid you'll have to put up with a certain amount of silliness of the sort Fujiwara's been suggesting."

"Our fault?" said Kagu, stifling a yawn. His skeptical tone was echoed by coughs from the half-dozen gray mugs who had just joined us. We had been trying to work out meeting arrangements for the past hour, partly on radio to Fujiwara, at sixty-five the youngest of the Ecological Syndics and, on Sally and Mummett's account, by far the wiliest of the "world leaders" on the embassage ship. Kagu was already bored and nettled.

"If," replied Mummett, "you hadn't brought us all the way from Trans-Pluto to Lagrange Five so quickly, they might have had more time to work out details of precedence, neutral territory, and so on."

"Make it worse," hooted Go-Candy, lips forming an O in her angelic, blue-eyed face, "give human more time, make more trouble." At peace for more than a hundred years, humanity had no official chain-of-command, nor any means of quickly acquiring one. The Ecological Syndics, the closest thing to a central authority, prospered through decision avoidance, ceremony, and indirection.

"As it is," said Mummett, "in a few minutes we'll have two-dozen high-muck-a-mucks here, running off in all directions with heroic postures, ready to take offense at almost anything, and dense-headed as the day is long. And without your bright suggestion, it'd be over a hundred."

Sally's bright suggestion had been the "neutral territory" of a silicon-laminate sphere, opening on one end into the torus, at the other into the "world leaders" ship. Like a circular table the inside surface of a sphere has no favored seating position, thus finessing issues of precedence, both among the humans, and between human and monkey. She easily beat down Fujiwara's radioed worry that his biggies wouldn't accept a monkey-made sphere as neutral and mutual. "Let the ship provide the air for the sphere. The side that brings the meat can't complain that the other supplies the plates."

The whirgirs could as easily have made a sphere large enough for thousands, but no reason to bandy that fact about.

"I'll have—am having—sufficient trouble," sighed Kagu, "convincing enough of us to show up to match the two dozen. Hard to attract anthropologists to this sort of ceremonial fatuity, and since your humans won't tolerate whirgirs as replacements, I have to call in all my favors to manage it."

"Durn tooting, bardner," piped Nod, who had just joined us, bringing the message that the sphere was ready for inflation. He was accompanied by his tall student friend and several other anthropologists. We had spent the last hour in a sort of temporary command center where Kagu had found us at air lock 4. Kagu had carried on both an animated conference with us and, at the same time, subvocalized, touch-typed, and monkey whistled to the various strata of Vineland. Now he had had it.

Our efforts to accommodate the arriving embassage had had a helter-skelter, lunatic aspect. I was glad it was over.

"Remember," pleaded Mummett, "not a word about us. Most of the world leaders don't even know about our unofficial visit. An open acknowledgement of our presence would make their position impossible in their own minds. They're supposed to be first, you understand. They have to be first."

Several gray mugs—no anthropologists, they—stared at Mummett.

"Fathers and mothers," I said, watching Kagu to make sure I had the tone right, "understand this as a cultural taboo. Senior minds should not be troubled by the antics of youngsters."

Kagu nodded yes to the gray mugs. "Senior egos," he whispered in my direction.

"Not a word," repeated Mummett. "Chancellor Household will speak first, because he's oldest. And try to follow the lead of Fujiwara. He'll be operating as a sort of protocol officer, rather than plenipotentiary."

The monkeys looked at him dubiously, like staid atheists invited into a revivalist tent for an ecstatic bout of speaking in tongues.

"Please," said Mummett, "it won't take long." The world leaders had reluctantly agreed to five minutes of remarks apiece, so, excepting Fujiwara who had no official speaking period, that meant two hours minimum human rhetoric. So Mummett was sugaring the pill. As it turned out, however, he was right.

Like a man whose pill wasn't sugared, Kagu pursed his lips and waved his colleagues forward into the neutral bubble. I followed Mummett, Sally, and Go-Candy, to the small compartment where they could watch the ceremony through one-way glass, invisible and silent guests to an occasion they did so much to bring about.

"I come in peace for all mankind," said Chancellor Harold Household. "Take me to your leader." His fruity voice quavered tremulously. His face was such a combination of confusion and sincerity that I decided he was completely serious. His eyes looked from his seat on the ship side of the sphere to the indistinguishable confusion of monkeys on the other.

Kagu stifled in himself the laugh that Go-Candy give vent to in our little spy box. Nod giggled into his hand and the gray mugs just looked blank.

"I have no leader," said Kagu, "I am just an anthropologist."

"Me, too," said Nod.

270

Chancellor Household goggled at Kagu, puzzled by Kagu's remark. But, as figurehead of Oxford University, he certainly knew about the professional specialty.

"Ah yes," said Household, brightening, "a university man like myself. Anthropology. Primitives running about naked. Cannibalism and bestial fertility rites, don't you know. You'll want to go to New Guinea, I expect."

I would have liked to know how the translator put that speech to the gray mugs who weren't anthropologists. Some looked quite baffled, while two or three had their "suck-alum" look. I hoped they weren't reevaluating their attitude toward Tau Ceti III. I saw the older student who had urinated at Nod and the other student revolutionaries so long ago. He would bear watching.

Sally gave me a concerned look, shaking her head. This could get bad.

"On this historic occasion," said Chancellor Household, having once more caught sight of his role, "of the first contact between our two peoples, two great galactic civilizations, I am proud to represent humanity in this supreme adventure."

"Captain," hissed one of Household's octogenerians, "ask who's captain, they've got to have a captain."

With the speaker in our spy box cranked up, we could not only hear that remark, but also the voice that crankily whispered, "They all look alike. Monkeys."

"Yes," agreed Household, "I address my remarks to your captain, and the leaders of your great civilization, who are as eager, I am sure, as we are for all the benefits that must flow from this historic event."

"Our 'captain,'" said Kagu, "is what you call a robot. As to the more prominent and powerful central figures in our civilization, I assure you that they cannot be eager, for they haven't heard of you and aren't likely to, unless they read specialist journals. I will, of course, continue to write up your people, and your rustic ways, for *Primitivity Review*." Kagu pronounced the last two words distinctly and slowly.

Now there were several reddening faces among the human biggies, that and coughs and mutters. One caught words like "insult," "sick joke," "outrage." More gray mugs sucked alum. And the older student stood up.

Sally leapt up and before the rest of us could move she was through the door into the bubble. I followed, figuring at least I could get in front of the monkey who was reaching for his penis.

"I am happy," said Sally, ostensively to the monkeys, "to report that we've repaired the basic damage to your vessel. Lucky, with your ship limping along so distant from your civilization. Humanity is glad to help victims of space disaster." She turned to the dumbfounded Kagu, before he could say anything, and took his shoulder solicitously. "And this poor injured sailor," she said shushing him, "who's been saying such odd things, like any shipwrecked soul. I trust he's begun to recover from his disorientation."

Now the humanly muttered words—with doubt and question rather than pure outrage— were "first contact," "victims," "impossible." Because of Sally's appearance, it couldn't be first contact. But it could be something else, something much less demeaning than primitivity.

"Now," said Sally to Fujiwara, "shall we take our distinguished visitors for their inspection of the damage to the alien craft?" She gestured to where the mirror assembly joined the crosspiece. Even untutored eyes could see there had been recent damage.

"Certainly," said Fujiwara quickly, "never has a more distinguished group met to assist unfortunate stranger. A credit to humanity."

"Hands across the galaxy," said Sally.

"The valiant leader of our rescue effort," I said, "has put his life on the line to save the alien ship. Now that we've repaired the damage we must rescue him. I'm sure that Lieutenant Fitzwilliam deserves the highest commendation for heroism and leadership." Hearing this on his broadband might well make pighead drop the word 'mutiny' from his vocabulary. May he swim in an ocean of medals.

Well, that was more or less it. Fujiwara's party departed happy, retrieving Fitzwilliam on their way back to Earth Sat.

"The leadership of Earth has conducted a difficult and dangerous inspection of the damaged alien craft after the heroic rescue effort of Lieutenant Fitzwilliam. It will be decades before the leadership of the alien culture will be able to travel the distance to Earth." That's what we heard on world viddie. That and Chancellor Household's mellifluent pronouncement that, "I will be proud to meet him then."

As part of the "hands across the galaxy" theme, Kagu, having recovered his sense of humor, agreed to tour the Earth as a poor spacewrecked castaway.

"Not a bad fate for an anthropologist," said Kagu. "I'm practicing savage grunts and a primitive idiot grin."

Leave-Taking _____

"**N**OT ALL of it, you understand, sir," said Kagu, his eyes light with laughter, "just the least bit. Another tale or two, a flourish of dance, an addition to the Generalization that you saw when last we talked here."

The rock garden, like much of the rest of Vineland outside the tech section, had a mussed and abandoned air, like a large living room left in the wake of two dozen five-year-olds. Bands of whirgirs, accompanied by scores of house-cleaning robots, were still bustling about the tech section. But aside from basics like the waterfall, they had yet to manicure here. Greeting formalities done, Sally and I leaned against rock in the center of the gravel expanse, eyeing the trackless blue expanse where Drink-The-Sky wheeled in Escherlike figure eights, always seeming to fall, while in fact rising. Where rock joined greenery, Go-Candy talked excitedly to copperman, who was once more the spindly toy. She had recruited two monkey geneticists, too, and the bunch were already talking return of the chimpanzee.

"I think," continued Kagu, "that *she* would like being part of the Generalization story."

"She?" My eyes turned from the sky to Sally.

"Sally, too, of course, of course. But you know who I mean, sir." Kagu bowed and walked off to refill Professor Mummett's glass. By the look of Mummett's ruddy, smiling face, he might not need much more. But then, this place was not much given to sobriety.

"Cadmus," said Sally, "teach me to fly. Tell my body a story."

I nodded, the tingle of eternity sparkling up my spine. If we lived together, you'd have to call it an extended family.

"But first tell me. And *I* want all of it."

Okay.